W9-AQO-036

THE FIGHTER

THE FIGHTER

JEAN-JACQUES GREIF

First published as *Le Ring de la Mort* in 1998 by École des Loisirs, Paris

Published by Bloomsbury Publishing, New York, London, and Berlin
Distributed to the trade by Holtzbrinck Publishers

Library of Congress Cataloging-in-Publication Data
Greif, Jean-Jacques.
[Ring de la mort. English.]
The fighter / by Jean-Jacques Greif. — 1st U.S. ed.
p. cm.
Summary: Moshe Wisniak, a poor Polish Jew, uses his physical strength and
cleverness, plus luck, to help him survive the horrors he is subjected to in the
concentration camps of World War II. Based on the life of Moshè Garbarz.
ISBN-10: 1-58234-891-X • ISBN-13: 978-1-58234-891-9
1. Holocaust, Jewish (1939–1945)—Juvenile fiction. [1. Holocaust, Jewish
(1939–1945) —Fiction. 2. Concentration camps—Fiction. 3. Jews—Fiction.] I. Title.
PZ7.G86242Fi 2006 [Fic]—dc22 2006001291

First U.S. Edition 2006
Typeset by Westchester Book Composition
Printed in the U.S.A. by Quebecor World Fairfield
10 9 8 7 6 5 4 3 2 1

Bloomsbury Publishing, Children's Books, U.S.A.
175 Fifth Avenue, New York, NY 10010

All papers used by Bloomsbury Publishing are natural, recyclable products
made from wood grown in well-managed forests. The manufacturing processes
conform to the environmental regulations of the country of origin.

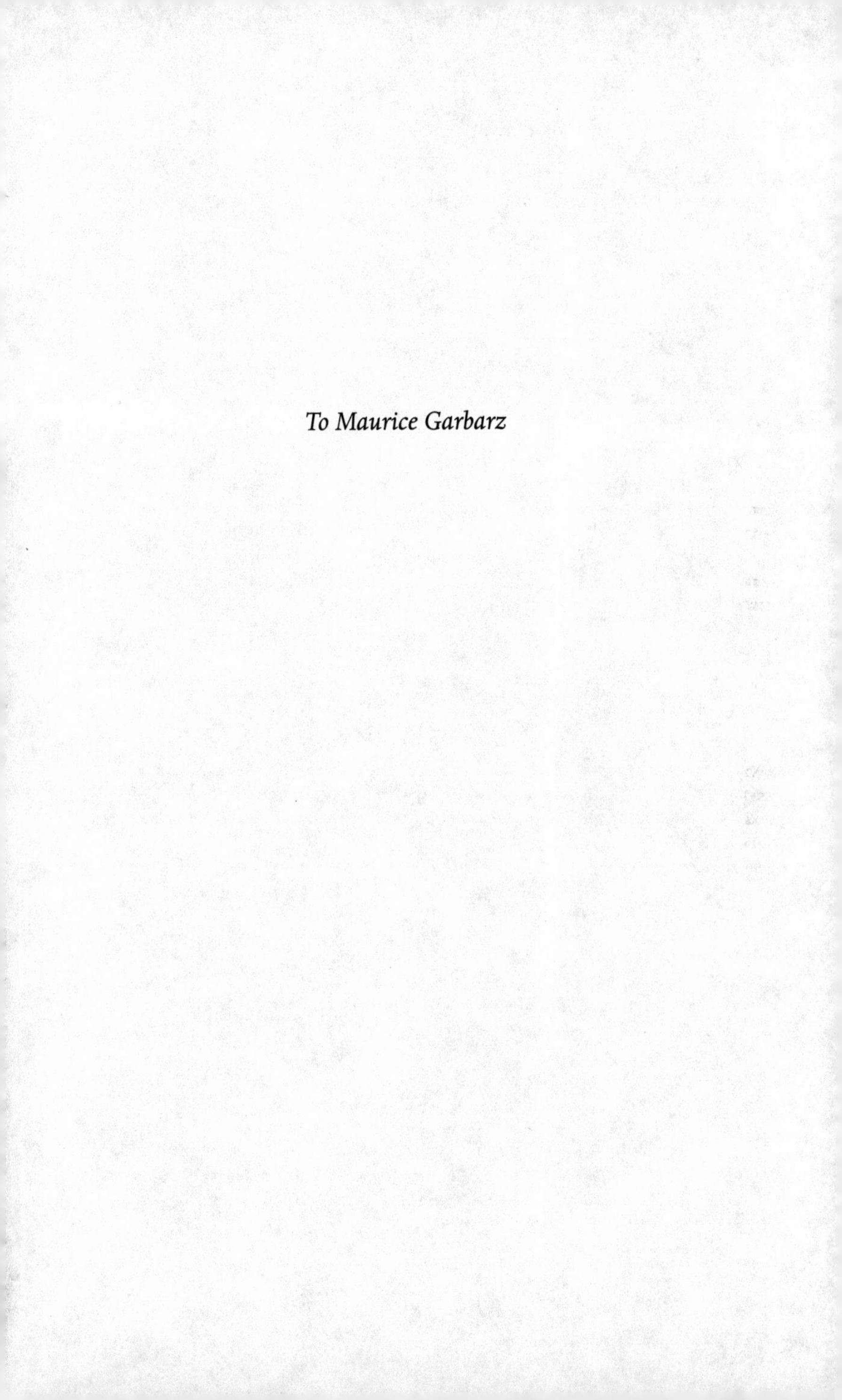

To Maurice Garbarz

THE FIGHTER

CHAPTER 1

1918. *In Praga, a suburb of Warsaw*

"Come, Moshe," my mother says. "In this new Poland, children have to be registered."

When I was born, the czar still reigned over the great Russian empire and Poland was a mere trinket hanging from his belt. He had so many subjects that nobody ever tried to count them. He didn't even ask them to register their children. Or, at least, he didn't ask my mother.

At the end of the First World War, the czar of Russia tumbled down from his throne. His army of Cossacks left Warsaw. Poland became an independent country.

We walk to the town hall in Praga, our Warsaw suburb.

"How many children?" the man in the office asks.

"What you say?"

"How many? Your children, lady!"

"Four children."

She finds him hard to understand. Before the war, the

government people spoke Russian. Now it's Polish. Why don't they ever speak Yiddish, the language of the Jews?

"How old are they?"

"Schmiel Yankl, my first, he more than ten, sir."

"More than ten years old?"

"Yes, sir."

"Okay, let's say eleven. I'll register him as Schmiel Yankl Wisniak, born in 1907. Next one?"

"My daughter, Pola Kailé, she younger."

"Of course. If he is your eldest. When was she born?"

"Schmiel, he walked already."

"Let's say he was two. Pola Kailé Wisniak, born in 1909."

"Then Anschel Leib come."

"Did the daughter walk already?"

"Hmm . . . Yes, sir."

"I'll write down Anschel Leib Wisniak, born in 1911. Is that all?"

"Also my last one, Moshe Azik."

"Two years later?"

"No, sir. He young . . ."

"Your youngest, I understand. All right: Moshe Azik Wisniak, born in 1913."

This is the date written on my birth certificate and all my other papers, but my mother is quite sure I was born on January 17, 1915. Who can know better than she? There was a great flu epidemic. My father died a few weeks after my birth.

Before my father's death, we were poor already. Afterward,

we became even poorer. My mother sews day and night near the window or under the light of the oil lamp. She is known as Myriam the Seamstress. Her customers can barely pay her. When I was a baby, as she didn't eat enough, her milk was too watery to nourish me. I was very small. My legs were so thin and crooked that I couldn't stand up. I sat on the floor all day. I moved, though: I glided around as fast as a stone on a frozen lake. Soon after my third birthday, my mother brought me to a healer—that is, a doctor who couldn't get a diploma on account of being a Jew.

"He has rickets," he said. "Give him two spoonfuls of cod-liver oil every day."

After a few weeks, I was strong enough to begin walking. Now they call me Monkey Moshe, because my legs are curved like a chimp's. I am very thin.

If it weren't for my brother Anschel, hunger would kill us all. He is clever. He sticks an iron pike at the end of a cane, then he steals potatoes on market days. On other days, he sits down in the street and weeps.

"Why are you crying?" people ask him.

"'Cause I'm hungry."

"Poor kid . . . Here, go and buy some food!"

They give him loose change. He buys bread and brings it home. My other brother, Schmiel, has a job already. He cuts leather for one of my father's cousins. He left school when he was ten, although he loved to study. Anschel will also leave school when he is ten. Already, he doesn't go too often, as he spends all day looking for food. The salesgirl at the grocer's takes pity on him. When he asks for a quart of milk, she fills up his can, which contains half a gallon. One day, the grocer's wife hears him buying half a quart of oil for the lamp. She comes out of her back shop and sees he is carrying a gallon-and-a-half jug.

"Oy, your mother gave you quite a big jug to carry just half a quart of oil. You seem to find it rather heavy. . . ."

My brother tells us about it.

"Lucky she didn't look inside the jug! It would have meant the end of my scheme."

Pola, my sister, finds him selfish.

"You think only about yourself. What about the salesgirl? She would have lost her job!"

We're always hungry. When Anschel brings home a potato, he divides it into eight parts. Food is so scarce that we rejoice when we eat one-eighth of a potato or two.

The market comes to our courtyard on Tuesdays and Fridays. It isn't a big one like they have in Warsaw. Peasants lay out their vegetables on the ground. They sell turnips, beetroots, beans, cabbage, pickled cucumbers in a bucket, homemade vodka—and above all, potatoes. The kids sing a ditty:

Sunday, potatoes
Monday, potatoes
Tuesday, potatoes
Wednesday and Thursday, potatoes

Friday, potatoes
Saturday, potato cake.

The courtyard is large, with houses on three sides and stables on the fourth. We live in a big room plus a small kitchen, on the second floor of a four-story building. At night, we stick two folding beds together and the five of us sleep there, as close as sardines in a can. They put me in the middle. In winter it's warm and cozy, but in summer I'm too hot.

They say that rich people have pipes that bring water into their homes. In our courtyard, people gather at the fountain all day long to fill up pitchers, jugs, tin cans. We keep water at home in a barrel. In winter, it freezes during the night.

Four outhouses stand in the courtyard, just under our window. I imagine that stinking gnomes live underground in a huge palace, the outhouses being its turrets.

I like to sit near the window. I watch the fountain, the outhouses, and especially the stables. They contain twelve carts, which are just simple wooden platforms drawn by two horses. I admire the skill of the carters when they tie mountains of scrap or rags on their platforms. Ah, these carters are tough men. Every evening, they get drunk on vodka in a filthy tavern on this side of the courtyard, then they cross back to the stables, singing and staggering, to sleep with their horses. Some of them are Jewish. I know we're Jewish, too, but I can barely understand them. The language they speak sounds like Yiddish, but it contains strange words. "It's slang," my mother says.

I notice that my brothers often come home with cuts and bruises all over their faces and bodies. Every other day, my mother sews up their old sweaters and their pants.

"The Poles attacked us," they say.

"We ran, but they caught us."

"They ambushed us at the corner."

Why do the Poles attack the Jews? That's a great mystery. For a long time, I thought that the word *Jew* actually meant "poor," but in fact these Poles who are not Jewish are often as poor as we are.

My brother Schmiel says that in Warsaw, on the other side of the Vistula River, the Jews live together in neighborhoods where the Poles do not enter. Our neighborhood, Praga, is "mixed," which means that we can't escape the Poles. We must be careful.

I stay at home because of my crooked legs, but I walk better now. I'll soon go out into the courtyard and the streets. I'll have to face theses terrible Poles. My brothers are cowards. As soon as they see a Pole, they run away. I won't give in. I'll fight. I'll be as strong as the carters. When a carter argues with a peasant, he comes right up to him and grabs the lapels of his jacket. The peasant falls to the ground right away. At first I didn't understand what happened. Then, after seeing many fights from my window, I noticed that the carter gave a knock with his head or a kick with his knee between the peasant's legs. The carter's move is so fast that you hardly see it. I'll grab the Pole by his jacket lapels and knock him out!

When the opponent knows how to fight, it is quite a different matter. Another gang of carters declares war on our guys. A battalion of enemies enters the courtyard. Our carters, Jews and Poles, confront the danger together. At first they fight with fists and feet. Then they grab sticks and chains. When these weapons fail, they pull out knives. The fighting lasts all night long. At dawn, we hear gunshots. My mother forbids me to go near the window, because of stray bullets. Once the fight is over, the police come to pick up the wounded and the dead.

Stray bullets are very dangerous. Mazik, the carters' leader, is a real thug. He levies his share of the cartloads, carries and resells stolen goods, extorts money from peasants who want to get a spot in our courtyard on market day. Sometimes he drinks so much he becomes crazy. He screams, waves his handgun, shoots everywhere. In the end, he puts his gun in his pocket and falls to the ground, dead-drunk. Then people find another body lying on the ground. It so happens that it is one of Mazik's enemies, someone who insulted him or didn't pay his due. The witnesses report the events to the police: Mazik was beyond himself, he was shooting without aiming. What could they make of it? The victim was killed by a stray bullet. Me, sitting near my window, I often see Mazik shooting at a target for practice. He staggers and lurches and waves his arms like a windmill. . . . A shot in the air, a shot on the ground, a shot in the center of the target!

Our Praga neighborhood is very poor. Everybody says it is a thieves' nest. From my window, I watch pickpockets at work on market days. You need good eyes to see more than a peasant jumping and hollering because his money has vanished. The pickpocket's hand is so fast. . . . It dives into the peasant's pocket and comes out holding a thick wallet. I see it! I also see something strange: just before the pickpocket acts, a man in a hurry jostles the peasant. After watching for weeks, I can follow the whole scene. The pickpocket needs three partners. Two of them shout at each other and trade insults, then pretend to fight. Gawkers gather right away. The third partner elbows his way through the crowd to reach the front row. As he pushes the peasant aside, he gives him a nasty poke in the back with his elbow. The peasant screams. He looks for the brute who hurt him so he can curse at him. He focuses his attention on the pain in his back. He doesn't feel the crafty caress of the pickpocket's hand.

Some robbers wait for the end of market day. Having sold all his vegetables, the peasant is going back to his village. He has bought cigarettes, candles, and other goods that the villagers have ordered. The robber jumps onto his cart noiselessly, rustles around in the bags to feel what they contain, then throws cigarette packs and candles to his accomplices. There is a saying in Yiddish: "The robber is so skilful that he would steal the crack of your whip."

As soon as my legs are strong enough, my brother Anschel finds work for me.

"You know all the thieves, Moshe. I'll introduce you to a peasant who'll give you a job as a guard."

"If I see a thief, I give him a headbutt!"

"You'd better not. You pull the peasant's jacket and show him the thief, that's all."

The peasant's eyes widen when he sees his new guard. I am five years old, but I am very small.

"This runt will protect my goods?"

"That's the whole point. The robbers won't notice him. They won't be very cautious, so he'll be able to spot them easily."

As I perform my task quite well, the peasant gives me three potatoes. A real treasure!

Resourceful Anschel has found an unlimited stock of food:

"The owner of the stables wants me to feed the horses. I told him you would help me. We can eat as much as we want."

"Horse food?"

"Potatoes. We grind potatoes and mix them with oats."

We can even put potatoes into our pockets and bring them home. The owner of the stables doesn't care. We cost much less than regular workers. I'm glad I'm using a spade and turning the grinder's crank. Since my legs are weak, I want to strengthen my arms. I have decided to become very strong. I lift up stones, I climb trees, I carry crates for the peasants.

Even when we gain weight, we still suffer from skin rashes because we don't get enough vitamins. That's one way you can know whether someone is poor: we poor people scratch ourselves all the time.

CHAPTER 2

Poles have a sixth sense

My mother wants to send me to public school. It's free, which is quite convenient. I'd learn to speak Polish. This might be useful later on. The principal warns her: "I can't guarantee his safety. You'd better send him to one of your own schools."

So I'm a pupil in the Jewish school. They don't ask us for tuition. How could my mother pay?

In the public school, the other kids would beat me to a pulp during recess. Here there is no danger—as long as I stay inside the walls. After school, I do have to walk home. The Polish schoolboys attack us on the way. With my crooked legs, I can't flee like the others. I try to catch a Pole by his lapels to give him a good butt. I'm much too small. My head comes to the level of his belly! Thanks to my small size, they take pity and don't hit me too hard.

I find a large bag that used to hold potatoes. I ask my

mother for small pieces of cloth to fill it up. I call it a punching ball. I hang it from the doorframe between our room and the kitchen. I hit it for hours every day. My brothers and my sister laugh at me. You won't laugh anymore when I'm champion of the world!

By and by, I grow up and the shape of my legs improves. When I'm seven, my uncle Prezman decides it's time I go to the synagogue with him. He replaces my father, who should have taken care of my religious education. My uncle picks a very solemn day: Yom Kippur, the day of atonement. The synagogue is right in our courtyard. It is just the first floor of one of the houses. It looks like a big store. It smells of cold tobacco and onions. It is full of smoke in winter, like the other houses, because they heat it with brown coal, which is cheaper. We must spend the whole day in this holy place, praying and fasting.

"Uncle Prezman?"

"Yes, Moshe."

"The other years, I used to eat on the day of Yom Kippur."

"You shouldn't have. At least this year you won't."

"Why, Uncle Prezman?"

"Moshe, you're spending the day inside the synagogue. This is the last place where you could eat something today."

"Hey, I think that I fast enough on other days!"

I get out of the synagogue and vow never to enter it again.

I fast so much that I faint in class. The school principal gives me bread and sweetened milk to get me back on my feet.

Despite hunger, I become very strong. When we practice wrestling, none of my schoolmates can beat me. Outside, when Poles attack us, I give them a taste of my headbutts and knee kicks. I also know a secret trick. I grab my opponent by his jacket lapels; I bend my knee and raise my foot to his stomach; I roll on my back, taking him down with me, then I let his jacket go and straighten my leg, throwing him back behind me. He usually stays on the ground for at least ten minutes. What's for sure is that he won't ever feel like bothering me again.

I still don't understand why the Poles hate the Jews. They shout, "Filthy Jews! Go back to your own land!" My land is Poland. My brother Schmiel, who is quite a scholar, says they mean to send us back to Palestine, where Jews lived two thousand years ago.

Their religious faith feeds their hate. If we want to remain alive, we'd better stay home when they march in the streets on a Sunday or a Catholic holiday. One Sunday, the son of the vodka seller walks out of the courtyard just as a religious procession is marching by. He is a poor simple-minded boy.

"Hey, you, are you Jewish?" some fellows who come at the tail of the procession ask him.

Instead of answering, he grins foolishly. The Poles think he is laughing at them. They start beating him up.

"Stop! Stop!" a tenant of the courtyard screams. "This is the son of the vodka seller. He isn't even Jewish!"

She runs to the police station. When she comes back with the cops, the child is dead already. The Poles didn't know what to make of his strange face. Otherwise, they have a kind of sixth sense that lets them recognize Jews. In their caricatures, they depict Jews with a big crooked nose, prominent black eyes, black frizzy hair—what they call the *Oriental type*. Me, I have red hair and blue eyes. Nevertheless, they know I'm Jewish. When I believed that *Jewish* meant "poor," I thought that they beat kids who walked barefoot, like my brothers and me. Then, before she sent me to school, my mother bought an old pair of shoes from a peddler for me. This didn't prevent the Poles from attacking me.

The Jews often sell clothes. Either secondhand clothes as peddlers, or new ones as tailors. My brother Anschel, after leaving school at ten like Schmiel, is now a tailor's apprentice. My sister, Pola, helps my mother sew.

Anschel worries all day long: where can he find some food? earn a little more money?

"Come here, Moshe. I'll take your measurements."

"Take my measurements? Why would you do that?"

"I'll cut a first-rate suit for you."

"Are you kidding? Where will you find cloth?"

"We'll buy a secondhand coat. I'll remove the most threadbare parts, then I'll cut a jacket in what's left. Since you're small, we won't need much. Then we'll go to Uncle Prezman. . . ."

"If we come at dinnertime, he may give us some food!"

"I won't refuse if he does, but I have another goal. When he sees your beautiful jacket, he'll order the same one for his son. He probably has an old coat or two somewhere. Then he'll talk to his friends, who'll order jackets next. We'll become rich!"

We buy the coat. I unstitch it carefully. Anschel cuts pieces for the jacket in the better-looking parts, just like he said he would. He has been an apprentice for three years. He is quite skillful.

I look like a little English lord in my superb new jacket. We go to Uncle Prezman, full of pride and hope. We're hardly out of the courtyard when we see two Poles at the other end of the street. Anschel doesn't like that.

"They're much taller than us. Let's bolt!"

"Come on, look, they're also wearing new clean suits. They won't fight."

Deep inside me, I hope that they won't take me for a Jew, since I don't seem poor anymore. Just when we pass them, one of them punches me in the stomach. When I fight, I can resist a blow to the stomach, but I was so far from expecting a fight that I fall backward, breathless. Anschel knows what to do: he runs away like a rabbit. The two

Poles begin to really hit me. Anschel is out of danger. He turns around, he wavers. Will he let two bullies knock his brother down right in front of him? And what about the suit, the new magnificent suit?

Yeah, he comes back to save his brother and his suit. The Poles see a taller fellow coming at them. They face him and get ready. They let me go. They think I've had enough and will flee. My good Anschel doesn't know how to fight. The Poles throw him to the ground within two seconds. Me, I have a little hook in my pocket, a kind of broken and sharpened key, a fine weapon. When I hold the key's buckle in my fist, the tip that appears between my fingers is almost invisible. One Pole pins my brother down with his knee. I lurch at him so fast that he can barely turn around and see what's happening. I give him a blow that rips his cheek in two as if it were paper. He screams with pain, falls to the ground, gets up and runs away. The second Pole shouts as loud but runs slower, because I opened his thigh with my key.

We give up our visit to Uncle Prezman and go home in awful shape. Anschel looks at me with wonder.

"Gosh, Moshe, you really taught them a lesson! One punch each. You're really strong. You'll have to show me how you do it."

"'Tis easy. I use my faithful assistant."

I show him my sharp key.

"Hey, man, you're crazy. This thing is dangerous. You could hurt someone."

"Of course. That's what it's for. I bet the bastards painted me a new face. Is my nose awfully bloody?"

"Well, there is blood. . . ."

"I feel like my eye is swelling up. Bah, in a few days I'll be like new. Fixing the suit will be harder."

"Don't worry. I'll stitch it back for you."

We wash the suit, Anschel mends it, then we go to Uncle Prezman. He doesn't order jackets for his children. He allows us to eat yesterday's leftovers in the kitchen.

The Poles are not my only enemies. One of the Jewish carters, Fat Yatché, has taken a dislike to me. They should call him Enormous Yatché. What with their thieving and bootlegging and trafficking, the carters do not suffer from hunger! They even eat meat several times a week. Fat Yatché hates all children, including his own. He lives with his wife, his daughter, and his son in a small house near the tavern. He's the only carter who doesn't sleep in the stables. He is so rich that he buys his water. We see the water carrier enter Yatché's house every morning, his two buckets hanging from a pole balanced on his shoulder. Yatché's son, who is already as fat, stupid, and brutal as his father, is always looking for a fight. You want it? You'll get it! My pals and me, we get together and drive some respect into his thick skull. Fat Yatché won't let anybody but himself whack his son. He would like to thrash all the boys in the courtyard, but he can't do that on account of their fathers. Thus, having no father to protect me, I'm the sole butt of his anger. I could write a song:

When Fat Yatché passes me,
on Sunday he gives me a blow,
on Monday a slap,
on Tuesday a slug,
on Wednesday a cuff,
on Thursday a chop,
on Friday a kick,
on Saturday a wallop.

Me, I'm bent on revenge. While Yatché is getting drunk in the tavern, I sneak behind his house and get his she-goat. I push her into the cesspool. The courtyard kids laugh themselves hoarse:

"Fat Yatché, Fat Yatché, your she-goat is taking a shit bath!"

Fat Yatché comes running. He fishes his she-goat out just before she drowns. She doesn't look good, not to mention the smell. Without taking time to ask anyone, he rushes into our building and climbs the stairs. Even if he doesn't suspect me, he may assume I've seen everything from my window. He'd enjoy torturing me until I inform against the offender. My mother knows that.

"Go to bed, Moshe. Quick!"

Fat Yatché is already knocking on the door and coming into the room.

"Where is that good-for-nothing son of yours? I have some questions to ask him about my she-goat."

"He is ill. See, he's been lying in this bed for two days. He has fever."

I don't need to pretend. I shiver for real and big drops of sweat run down my face.

Fat Yatché lives real close to the tavern, but he can barely walk home when he's really drunk. One winter evening, he slips on a sheet of ice and breaks his skull. He falls into a coma and dies five days later. Now, no one watches over his son. When his father used to hit me, the big dummy would add a few smacks of his own just because he felt safe. Well, things have changed, fatso! I pass him in the courtyard. Just out of habit, he hits me in the ribs. I raise my guard and shout, so that the whole courtyard can hear me:

"You want to fight, big barrel of piss? Well, let's fight."

A crowd gathers around us. Yatché's son draws his knife. He is two years older than me and a head taller, but I'm not afraid. I don't even need my little piece of steel. I'll fight empty-handed, fair and square. I move forward suddenly. . . . He lowers his right hand to stab me in the stomach. I didn't plan to impale myself on his knife: my move was a trick! I only wanted him to bring his hand within my range. I move back and kick it hard. The shoes my mother bought from the peddler are heavy hobnailed boots. My kicks hurt like hell! His knife falls to the ground. Before he can pick it up, I grab the lapels of his jacket. The crowd cheers me:

"Come on, Moshe!"

"Kill him!"

"Show him what you can do!"

I show him some of my tricks: headbutt to the nose, knee kick to the groin, elbow poke into the eye. I explain the new rules.

"You'd better stay away from me. And don't come near my brothers, either!"

Fat Yatché's widow looks like an elephant. They call her *Mama Hinde*, that is Mama Gazelle, for fun. She is furious when she sees her son come home covered with blood. How can she accept this? Doesn't she belong to the courtyard's best circles? We hear her heavy step on our staircase. My mother opens the door.

"Is your son, the murderer, here? I'll kill him!"

My mother doesn't dare answer, she's so scared of Mama Hinde. I go to the kitchen and get the ax we use to cut wood for the stove. I come back into our room, ax in hand.

"Go away, Mama Hinde! Old witch! If you ever come here again, I'll split your head open, and then I'll take care of your son!"

My mother can't stand violence. She weeps.

"Oh, ma'm, go away quickly . . . I've never seen him in such a state. He'd really kill you!"

Mama Hinde goes down to the courtyard.

"The son of Myriam the Seamstress tried to crack my head. He's a crazy demon!" she shouts around.

My mother takes me into her arms and compliments me.

"With a protector like you, nobody will ever bother us anymore. But you really scared me with your ax."

CHAPTER 3

Only a revolution . . .

In 1926, soon after my eleventh birthday (if I was born in 1915), I leave school. My brothers call me lucky, because I stayed there for one more year than they did. Me, lucky? I become a cabinetmaker's apprentice in Warsaw, but I don't learn anything, except how to saw logs twelve hours a day. Good for my arms! To go home to Praga, I must walk across the Vistula. In winter, it is so cold that they have to install small coal stoves every fifty feet on the long bridge. I glide on the ice like a skater from one stove to the next. I have to rub my ears all the time, otherwise they'll freeze in spite of my woolen cap. I often see blue corpses in the middle of the bridge.

When the weather improves, I stop along the way to write slogans on the walls: *Down with fascism! Freedom! Let's say no to anti-Semitism!* My brother Schmiel explained it to me: only a communist revolution can put an end to the plight of the Jews.

"Communism means equality for all human beings. In fact, in the Communist Party, Poles and Jews fight together."

"In Russia, there was a revolution?"

"Yes. In 1917."

"So now they let the Jews alone?"

"Of course!"

As I am too young to become a communist militant, I join a group of "pioneers" or young communists. I find it rather strange that nearly all the pioneers are Jewish. When my brothers and I put up posters in the middle of the night, the people who attack us call us stinking Jews without even seeing our faces.

This same year 1926, Marshal Pilsudski leads a military coup, becomes a dictator, and bans the Communist Party. I demonstrate against the ban with thousands of other people. Horse-riding policemen charge at us, kill seven workers with their swords, wound hundreds. I succeed in running away, but I see the gleam of the swords for weeks in my nightmares. My brother Anschel is not so lucky. The police catch him writing slogans on a wall. He spends several months in jail.

My uncle Hersch Wisniak, my father's brother, used to dream of revolution, too. He took part in the series of riots that shook the Russian empire in 1905. Then he fled abroad before the police could catch him and deport him to Siberia. At first he lived in Germany, then he settled in Paris, and now he has a small leather business there. My mother writes a long letter to him:

> *My dear Hersch,*
>
> *I write to you in order to give you news of your nephews and niece. My last-born, Moshe, just left school to become an apprentice with a cabinetmaker. He likes to fight, but doesn't get into real trouble. His brother Anschel is a tailor's apprentice. He already knows how to cut a full suit. Pola, your niece, helps me with my stitching and sewing. She doesn't have a boyfriend yet.*
>
> *I want to tell you about Schmiel, my firstborn. As you know, he is a leatherworker, just like you. He works for my cousin Layb. He has been cutting and stitching leather for a long time. He has even designed several ladies' handbags. I think he could help you in Paris. Here, I fear for him, because he'll soon reach the age for military service. You remember that the Russians didn't take Jews into their army. Now the Poles take Jews, but then the other soldiers bother them and beat them. He is a very serious boy. I'm sure that you'll be satisfied with him if you let him come to Paris.*

Uncle Hersch's business is quite successful, so he needs new workers. Thus, he sends a French visa for his nephew. My mother, my sister, and me, we go to the railway station with Schmiel in January 1927. Anschel can't come with us, since he's still in jail. My mother imagines all kinds of mishaps.

"Paris is a very big city. There must be anti-Semites everywhere. Be careful!"

"Of course, Mama. Don't worry."

"How will you find your uncle? If you got lost in the streets of Paris, oy, it would be awful. . . ."

"Don't you remember? He wrote he'd come to the station."

"Yes, I remember now. You'll recognize him easily—he looks like your poor father. Take care not to catch a cold!"

My sister pulls my brother's sleeve:

"Schmiel, Schmiel, promise you'll write to me. . . . You must describe very precisely what ladies wear in Paris. Then I can create dresses according to the latest Paris fashion!"

"I'll write to you all. I'll earn lots of money and I'll send for you."

CHAPTER 4

My mother becomes the courtyard's queen

My dear Mama, my dear Pola, my dear Anschel (if you're out of jail), my dear Moshe,

I hope your health is as good as mine. The trip took a long time. I spent two nights on the train but didn't sleep much. I wondered what my new life would be like. We crossed Germany and Belgium. The north of France is gray and dreary. When I stepped out of the train, several well-dressed gentlemen addressed me in Yiddish. They wanted me to work in their leather business. They all promised me good wages. I saw Uncle Hersch standing nearby. I recognized him right away, like Mama said I would. I told the gentlemen I already had a boss. Uncle Hersch explained to me why this welcoming party waited for the Warsaw train every day: so many Jewish leatherworkers have settled in Paris that France is now exporting ladies' handbags everywhere. Demand is booming. They can't make enough of them. Anschel (if you're out of jail) and Moshe, you must definitely learn how to cut and stitch leather. Then you can come here.

Paris is a wonderful city: Would you believe that nobody attacks Jews in the streets? People don't even seem to guess I'm Jewish. Uncle Hersch did advise me to take a French name, so as not to tempt them. So now my name is Jacques. He is Henri.

My dear Pola, I live in a poor neighborhood. I work so hard that I haven't had time to visit the smarter parts of town. So I can't tell you what the elegant Paris ladies wear.

Mama, I gave a little memento to Baruch Seligman, a leatherworker who is traveling to Warsaw. He should bring it to you quite soon.

Your Jacques

The two last words are written from left to right, in French, which seems very refined to us. To write Yiddish, we use Hebrew letters and read them from right to left. As we don't know how to pronounce this strange name (Yakuhess?), we'll keep on saying Schmiel! The Paris memento that Baruch Seligman brings us is a twenty-dollar banknote.

When he comes out of jail, Anschel refuses to follow his elder brother's advice.

"I'm a tailor. I cut beautiful pieces of woolen cloth. It is a job that requires skill and good taste. I won't become a cobbler or whatever just because ladies' handbags sell well."

"Leatherworker is not the same thing as cobbler."

"Listen, Mama, I don't want to go to Paris. Do you think all Jews should leave Poland? The Poles say we do not belong in this country. This would confirm their slander. I must stay here to help the party start the revolution, since Schmiel quit his post."

In any case, I stop sawing boards at the cabinetmaker's. Wearing my nice suit, I go to Cousin Layb, the leatherworker. To make sure he takes me as an apprentice, I agree to work without being paid. Schmiel sends us dollars from France, so we have enough money for food.

I'm the new guy, so my cousin's employees would like me to be their errand boy and servant. "Moshe, go get me a piece of bread! Bring me some water!" The other apprentices have to obey them if they want to earn their wages. Me, I expect no salary, so I'm free. I know plenty of curses, I have strong fists, I don't let them boss me around. I learn how to cut leather with a special gouge that I must constantly sharpen on a stone. I can soon stick and curl, then "hemstitch" a piece of leather. I make small pieces: purses and wallets. By and by, my fingers become good judges of leather quality. Cousin Layb says I'm quite skillful. He shows me how to rivet leather to the metal clasp of a ladies' bag. This is delicate work. A good riveter earns four times as much as a regular worker.

I create a new style of wallet with paper and cardboard. I show it to a designer. He laughs at me:

"You're just an apprentice. Come see me in ten years!"

. . .

Does Anschel want to go back to jail? He spends his nights putting up posters on the walls. How long can it last? One night, the police turn up while he's at it. Luckily, he is clever—and learned a trick or two during the months he spent behind bars. He throws his bucket of glue and his posters over the wall, then begins to kiss the girl he's working with as if they were lovers. The cops don't know what to think. They take him to the police station. They lack any incriminating evidence. They let him go, but they warn him:

"If we catch you again, you stinking Jew, we'll play some games that you won't enjoy!"

It's very dangerous for a Jew to be "known by the police." They can send him to jail for years under some false accusation or even kill him without bothering about the law. So Anschel changes his mind about Paris. While he's waiting for Schmiel to obtain a working permit and send a train ticket, he stays at home. I bring him leather and some tools. I teach him the basics. Having such a fast learner as a student is a real pleasure. He's even more skillful than me!

. . .

One year after Schmiel, Anschel takes the train to Paris. My mother becomes the queen of the courtyard. Two sons in France, and they send American dollars every month! Everybody here knows we'll soon go and join them. We're angels ready to fly to paradise.

We take the train in May 1929. I am fourteen years old (even if my passport says sixteen). We carry huge bales, tied with miles of string. My mother and Pola need to bring their sewing machines, of course, but my mother also wanted to take her crockery and cutlery. We didn't leave anything in our apartment except the table and beds. We're moving, we're emigrating, we're leaving Poland forever.

During the long journey, we speak of the past and the future. In Poland, we were treated like strangers. We risked our lives every time we left our courtyard. There was no hope and plenty of fear. In Paris, we'll really be strangers. We'll have to learn French. We'll need to work hard.

The train is full of people. We spend thirty-six hours sitting on our bales. Ten minutes before coming into Paris, we see small houses with vegetable gardens, warehouses, factories, garages—suburbs similar to Warsaw's.

"Look, Pola, all the streets are paved!"

"You'll have to give up your favorite pastime, wallowing in mud!"

"Oh, look, a motorcar! Do you think all the French people own motorcars?"

"Don't be stupid! France may be more modern than Poland, but it isn't America."

The train rolls slowly under the high vault of the railway station. It slows down and stops. Brakes and steam emit loud shrieks. We step down onto the platform with our bales. My mother runs toward two well-dressed gentlemen.

"Schmiel! Anschel! I am so happy to see you again!"

"My name is Jacques, Mama."

"I'm Albert."

My brother doesn't pronounce his name Yakuhess, but something like Zhak.

"Wow, Moshe, you've grown up since I saw you last! You'll have to take a French name. Maurice, perhaps. That's close to Moshe. Pola, you'll become Paule. Mama, you'll always be Mama! You've brought too much luggage. I told you to stick to what was strictly necessary. I don't know where we'll put all this stuff. . . . Albert, take Mama's package."

"Albert? Who's this Albert? I won't let someone I don't know carry my bag."

"It's me, Mama, your son! Have you already forgotten my French name?"

My brothers used to share a tiny room. To accommodate us, they've moved.

"We found a bigger room for the whole family—in the nineteenth arrondissement of Paris, near La Villette."

As it is not very far from the railway station, we walk there. We climb six flights of stairs with the sewing machines and the bales full of crockery. The room is ten feet long by ten feet wide. Pola, I mean Paule, can't help laughing.

"This is your 'bigger' room? The other one must have been really tiny! I've heard that French people have water taps inside their homes. Where is it, this wonderful water tap?"

"Well, ahem, it is in the courtyard. The toilets, too."

"Let me see whether I get it right. It is just like Praga, except over there we had to climb down one flight of stairs to get water, whereas here we climb down six."

It really looks like our Praga home. We even use two folding beds in the same manner. When one of us wants to pee in the middle of the night, he has to step over the others to get out.

Before we came, Albert made bags and wallets with Uncle Henri (whom my mother still calls Hersch). He had also taken another job, with a tailor named Brod, in order not to lose his main skill. He went there in the evening. Now I take his place with Uncle Henri and he works for the tailor full time.

My mother and Paule find as much sewing work as they want. They install their sewing machines on a small table. When we come home, Jacques and I put the sewing machines away. The first thing we do is eat our dinner on the table. Then we use it to make wallets. The pieces of leather that we bring home are already cut. Paule helps us curl and hemstitch them. We earn so much money that we eat meat every other day, just like rich people. In Poland, it was once a month when business was good. It doesn't take long for Paule to become finicky:

"Here, chicken doesn't taste as good as at home."

"This is home!"

"You know the joke: *When does the poor Jew eat chicken? When either one of them is sick!*"

CHAPTER 5

Here, nobody guesses we're Jewish

A certain very clever lady has produced residence permits for us as if by magic. It takes three or four months for Jacques and Albert to pay her off. Then we earn enough money to rent another small room in the same building, which we use as a kitchen and a dining room. Now we can unpack our crockery and cutlery!

In the spring of 1930, nearly one year after our arrival, we feel so rich that we decide to take Sunday afternoons off.

"Come," Jacques says, "I'll show you a beautiful public park nearby. It is called *Les Buttes Chaumont.*"

While my mother and Paule prepare the Sunday chicken, I go out with my two brothers for my first walk in Paris. On rue Armand-Carrel, I see five tall fellows coming toward us.

"There's five of them against three of us. They seem strong. We'd better cross to the other side of the street. Quick!"

"Are you crazy, Moshe? After a whole year, you still think you're in Poland! Nobody guesses we're Jewish here. They don't even attack Jews."

In 1931, we move into a gigantic apartment near the boulevard de Belleville. We switch from the nineteenth to the twentieth arrondissement. We have two rooms, a kitchen, running water! We no longer have to climb down to the courtyard, since there are toilets out in the hallway.

Jacques and Albert speak a little French. I don't. I haven't met many Frenchmen. I don't even work at Uncle Henri's place anymore. As Jacques finds me skillful and fast, he brings a stitching machine for me in our new apartment. Thus, I can work for several bosses. I make handbags from seven in the morning until ten at night. I don't go out much. I curl, I stitch, I do everything from A to Z. These bags are pouches with a flap but no clasp: cheap stuff. I don't have to rivet, which is the toughest work.

I soon earn enough money to reduce the length of my workday. After all the hours I spend at my machine, I unwind in a sports club called YASC (Yiddische Arbeter Sporting Club*—Jewish Workers' Club). I go there every other evening and on Sunday. They also have conferences on Saturday afternoon, usually on communism and the Soviet Union. Over there, they don't exploit workers and don't

---

***Arbeter* is the Yiddish word for worker. In German, it would be *Arbeiter*.

persecute Jews. I would like to enroll in the Communist Party, but I can't run the risk. The French might decide to expel me as a "subversive foreign plotter" or something.

On Sunday, I often go to the countryside with my friends from the sports club. The YASC actually belongs to a bigger organization, FSGT (*Fédération Sportive et Gymnique du Travail*—Workers' Sports and Gymnastics Federation), which is close to the Communist Party. They rent meadows near Paris where workers can go and camp on weekends. I learn my first few words of French from communist factory workers on the banks of the Marne River. I also meet Polish Jews who are not tailors or leatherworkers, but medical students. They come from the better neighborhoods of Warsaw or from the parts of Poland that belonged to the Austrian empire before the Great War. Jews there were not as poor as in the Russian empire. They study medicine in France because the Polish universities limit the number of Jewish students. Their parents send them money, so they don't need to stitch wallets. When we play volleyball on the campgrounds, they can hardly hit the ball. They're thin and delicate. Some of them don't even speak Yiddish, but only Polish. The French would call them bourgeois. They did suffer for being Jewish, though, just like me, and believe, also like me, that the communist revolution will end our troubles.

I learn how to swim in the Marne River. I play volleyball and basketball. My favorite sport, however, is boxing.

I remember the day I entered the YASC's gymnasium, near the Place de la République, for the first time. Some guys were hitting a punching ball. Others were fighting. It was wonderful. It looked like dancing! My fists had been idle since I'd left Poland. I wanted to imitate these guys right away. The boxing teacher, a German Jew named Karl, gave me some gloves.

"You try to hit my face or my body. We'll see what you're worth."

"I won't hit too hard."

"Don't worry about that. Hit as hard as you want."

I am small but strong. He's a shrimp of a guy, with about as much muscle as a jellyfish. I was afraid I'd hurt him.

I couldn't hit him even once. He dodged all my blows, as if he figured them out in advance. After a few minutes, or maybe only thirty seconds, I was out of breath. I couldn't fight anymore. He could have knocked me down with a mere slap if he'd wanted to. He laughed.

"You're quite gifted. You give many punches. You've got lots of energy. How old are you?"

"Sixteen."

"If you work hard, you'll become a good boxer."

I follow his advice. I work hard. I jump rope to improve my legwork. Three minutes of jumping, then I rest and start again. Twelve times three minutes. I lie on my back and I do exercises to strengthen my abdominal muscles. I hit the punching bag "Faster!" Karl shouts. "Harder!" I hang a punching bag in our apartment, like I'd done in Warsaw. Except it is now filled with sand, rather than with pieces of cloth.

Before fighting against a real live opponent, I learn to move in a series of jumps: sideways, forward, backward, with a rotation or a twist. Karl teaches me to dodge blows by moving my head backward, by rotating, by crouching. I parry with my fists and my forearms, which become as hard as steel. I already know how to give and take punches, but I must work a lot to improve my dodging.

When I fought in the streets of Praga, I used to just hit whoever was in front of me. Karl tells me there's more to boxing than straight punches. He shows me other ones. The hook goes around your opponent's guard. The uppercut, when aimed carefully upward at your opponent's chin, knocks him out cold.

If both guys know how to fight, they'll avoid a knockout. They try to land a punch and count one point. During the first months, my score stays at zero. None of my punches ever connect.

"You shouldn't announce your moves in advance," Karl says.

"What do you mean?"

"Just before you hit, I see you move your arm and grin ever so slightly, so I can guess you're getting ready to let one go. You must learn to throw your fist as if you didn't think about it."

My first official fights take place in the club's gymnasium. I lose them all. My opponents just land more punches, so that they win on points. Then, by and by, I begin to win a fight now and then. After two or three years, I'm good enough to go to amateur tournaments with the club's team. As I weigh 108 pounds (being five foot three), I belong to the flyweight category. We fight in a gymnasium or a public hall, in front of a crowd that shouts and whistles at us. I'm good at hitting and parrying, but I'm especially good at thinking while I'm fighting. I look at my opponent, I size him up, I zero in on his weak points, and I knock him down. I always stay on my feet.

I don't consider becoming a pro. I like boxing, but not enough to make a life of it. People also say that professional boxing is controlled by gangsters and that matches are often fixed.

My biggest fight is against Nab, amateur flyweight champion of Paris. I feel rather nervous. This guy has fought so many different boxers that he'll find out how to beat me in no time. My teammates shout, "Crush him, Maurice!" As soon as we begin, I see it's not his day. He isn't exactly slow, but he reacts with a slight delay when I feint, so I succeed in landing a hook to his liver and several other good punches. At the end of the second round, I am several points ahead. He hates to lose, though. In the third round, he finds hidden strength somewhere and hits me twice in the face. He doesn't even seem to be trying hard. In the end, the match is a draw. If I had won and the title had been in play, I would have become champion of Paris!

I also fight in the street just like in the good old days.

The French people may hate Jews less than the Poles, but they did accuse a Jewish officer, Captain Dreyfus, of spying. As they had no proof, they made up a false telegram or something and convicted him. Many Frenchmen knew he was innocent. Others considered all Jews guilty. This was such a big event that Jews still talked about it twenty years later in our small corner of Warsaw.

These people who hate us say the Great Depression that followed the 1929 stock market crash in America is due to some kind of Jewish plot. Stupid politicians and journalists pretend that the best way to find work for jobless Frenchmen is to send foreigners, and especially Polish Jews, back to their own countries.

"This is just plain wrong," Jacques says. "We actually developed the market for handbags, so we brought more work for everybody and more money for France."

Thugs who admire Hitler and his Nazis have formed "leagues." A bunch of them roams our Belleville neighborhood. We call them Coats, because they wear long raincoats in order to hide clubs and other weapons. They recognize Jews sitting at outdoor cafés easily, since we're speaking either Yiddish or heavily accented French. They shout, "Down with the Jews!" and attack us with their clubs.

We boxers have decided to organize a counterattack. A Romanian Jew named Noika, who boxes well and runs even better, sips a coffee with a pal while speaking Yiddish loudly. The Coats come and begin to insult them in the usual way. Noika stands up and lands a heavy punch on the nose of the nearest fascist. Then he runs away, with the whole group of Coats trying to catch him. He doesn't run too fast, because he doesn't want to outpace them. All of a sudden, he slips through a door as if to vanish. This door belongs to an old Parisian building with a large archway for carriages. The Coats enter after him, hoping to give him a good beating in the archway. That's just where we're waiting for them. . . . They rush in, pushing and squeezing, so that tripping them is kid's play. Some fall flat on their faces and knock themselves out on the pavement. Others are frozen stiff with surprise. Although there are ten of us against twenty of them, we snatch their clubs without much effort and give them a taste of their own medicine.

After this reversal, the Coats stop coming to our neighborhood, but the cops start checking our ID papers all the time.

"Either the Coats and the cops are friends," Jacques says, "or they have mutual friends."

I'm lucky, I have a legal working permit as an apprentice leatherworker. Jacques also owns a precious worker's card, which he got when he came to France. This was before the

Great Depression. Albert, Paule, and my mother, who have residence cards but no working permit, could be expelled. When the cops come to check his boss's workshop, Albert hides in a closet.

CHAPTER 6

She speaks French like a real Parisian girl

In the spring of 1935, I meet Rachel during a camping weekend. She was born in France, but her parents are Polish Jews. She speaks Yiddish like us and French like a real Parisian girl, which amazes me. I find it fantastic that a Jewish woman, belonging to our people, looks like one of these fascinating Paris *femmes* whom we pass in the streets. Although my sister Paule (who is the only other young woman I know, actually) follows the latest fashion when cutting dresses for herself, she doesn't look as refined as Rachel. She's jealous.

"Well, my dear Maurice, it seems this dame has cast a spell on you! Beware: not everything that glitters is gold. . . ."

"What are you talking about? She's just a friend. We see things the same way. She hates the fascists and admires the Soviet Union, like me. She teaches me French. When

I don't understand a sentence, she can explain it to me in Yiddish."

"She's kissing your feet because you're a boxer. Women love boxers."

"I can introduce you to my pals at the club, if you want to kiss their feet!"

Before long, Rachel becomes more than a friend. Before the end of the year, we marry in the nineteenth arrondissement's municipal hall. The marriage certificate says we're both twenty-two years old, but of course I'm only twenty. We move into a room and kitchen two blocks from my mother's apartment. My brother Jacques, who got married a little before me, also lives in the same neighborhood. Albert and Paule stay with my mother.

Rachel supervises deliveries for a company that sells women's hats. She takes evening courses to become a typist. We're not millionaires, but we have saved enough money to go to a furniture store, Galeries Barbès, and buy a fantastic modern invention, a "convertible." In the daytime, it is a large comfortable sofa. At night, we push the dining table near the window, we put the chairs on top of it; then we unfold the sofa, which becomes a king-size bed. The mechanism is very clever. I would never have thought to use springs and levers in such a way. Otherwise, I made everything: the table, the chairs, the shelves.

"Did you saw wood in your courtyard in Warsaw?" Rachel asks.

"No, but I worked for a cabinetmaker."

I saw, I plane, I drill holes, I chisel, I fit parts, I paint, I varnish. I'm what they call a do-it-yourselfer. Poor people must always do things themselves. How else? I enjoy repairing a dripping faucet or replacing a fuse.

You turn the handle and water flows. You push a button and the lamp lights up. What wonderful inventions! Rachel laughs at me.

"You're like a country bumpkin who's never seen a modern home."

"I saw my uncle Prezman's place in Warsaw, but we had neither running water nor electric power at home. Coming to France was a good decision. I am living like a rich man!"

A big event takes place in 1936. A Jew, Léon Blum, becomes prime minister of France. I can't imagine such a thing happening in my home country. On the contrary, Poland is expelling all Jews from the government and public service, just like the Nazis did as soon as they seized power in Germany. New waves of anxious Jews arrive in Paris every day. The anti-Semitic leagues and newspapers grow more virulent.

The Léon Blum government, supported by the People's Front, an alliance of the socialist and Communist parties, forces the bosses to give two weeks of paid vacations to their workers. I'm not an illegal worker anymore, but a legitimate employee of my uncle, so I'm entitled to vacations like everybody else. We spend our two paid weeks camping in the Jura Mountains with *Les Amis de la Nature* (Nature's Friends), a new offshoot of FSGT. I am taking vacations for the first time in my life!

I think I'm happy, or at least happy enough. I live in a small but comfortable apartment with the woman I love. I'm not hungry. I have lots of friends, whom I see in the evening at the club and on Sundays when we camp on the banks of the Marne River.

. . .

In 1938, I'm twenty-three. I've been boxing for seven years. As Karl's assistant, I give lessons to newcomers. One day, Karl brings a young guy to me and asks me to see what he's worth.

"Okay. Go get some gloves and try to hit me. What's your name?"

"Rosenberg."

"I'm Wisniak. How old are you?"

"Fifteen."

This kid is even shorter than me. Five feet one, at most. I remember my first day at the club . . . I was in the same position, in front of Karl. I fought so hard that I forgot to breathe, but I couldn't hit Karl even once. Now it's my turn to jump aside and dodge with a smile on my face. Ha, but it isn't that easy . . . Shorty pretends he is a machine gun. He hits with both hands, any which way, without thinking. I don't smile anymore. I parry, I jump, I dodge. I hope he'll run out of breath! Well, I sock a few to his stomach to cool him down. This makes him furious! After a while, he does stop, utterly exhausted. With all this crazy shooting, one of his punches grazes my jaw. When I come home, Rachel shrieks to high heaven.

"Why, Maurice, did you look at yourself in a mirror? Your face is totally mangled!"

"My jaw is slightly out of line, but it'll straighten out. That's what you call an occupational hazard."

"Listen, you can't keep this up. It's a dangerous sport. You're the head of our family. Soon, you'll be a father. You have to start acting responsibly."

I don't always obey Rachel. I've got to admit that she has more common sense than me, though. She is pregnant. I'd better stop worrying her by being so foolish. I agree to hang up my gloves. I've boxed plenty anyway. I can't count my victories. Karl said I had the fists and the legs of a champion, but that something was lacking in my temper: savagery, rage, fierceness. I didn't really want to hurt my opponent. I saw several fights with the world champion Marcel Cerdan. Out of the ring, he's quite a sweet guy, full of charm, but when he fights he becomes a wild dog. As if he hated his opponent for some reason and was actually trying to kill him.

My brother Jacques says the reason I am not nasty enough is that I had no father.

"Do you know Doctor Freud?"

"I don't know any doctor. My health is good, thank God."

"He isn't a doctor in Paris, but a great scientist who lives in Vienna. He invented psychoanalysis. Haven't you heard of it?"

"I guess I may have. There was an article about this psychowhatsis in *Die Naïe Presse* the other day, but I didn't read it."

"According to this theory, boys love their mother and are jealous of their father. They don't know it, because these feelings are hidden in their subconscious mind. That's what Freud calls the Oedipus complex. They want to kill their father and marry their mother, like the Greek hero Oedipus."

"Nobody does that."

"Of course not, but all the boys want to do it in their subconscious mind. Since they can't kill their father, they take revenge on other men. When Marcel Cerdan tries to knock out the other guy, he is hitting his father without being conscious of it. You didn't have a father, so you don't want to hurt your opponents."

I don't know where Jacques finds all these strange theories. Or rather, I know quite well: in books he reads after work. While I practice sports to relax, he reads. I read only *Die Naïe Presse*, a Jewish newspaper with a communist bent, which has been around since 1934. Jacques says Paris is a fantastic city, where you can find a free public library in every municipal hall. When I stop boxing, I begin reading books like he does. I can't read French books, so I borrow books in Yiddish from the club's library: our great Jewish writers Peretz, Sholem Aleichem, Shalom Asch; translations in Yiddish of novels by Tolstoy, Gorky, Upton Sinclair, Maupassant.

Jacques has a daughter named Rose, born in 1937. At least she won't be jealous of him and try to kill him, like this Oedipus. My brother Albert is also married and he has a daughter, too.

Léon Blum has governed France for only one year. In 1938, a new cowardly government signs a treaty in Munich that lets Germany gobble up part of Czechoslovakia. It's obvious that Hitler won't stop there. We're afraid there will be a terrible war.

On May 15, 1939, we welcome our little Élie into this world.

CHAPTER 7

The Germans pound the streets of Paris with their heavy boots

On September first, 1939, the Germans bomb Warsaw and invade Poland. France and England, as Poland's allies, declare war on Germany.

An amateur boxing match lasts only three rounds. You climb into the ring and start punching each other right away. A big professional fight, in ten or fifteen rounds, is a different thing. Often, not much happens during the first round. The boxers move forward and backward, try a punch or two, dodge, and wait. This is called an observation round. In the great fight between France and Germany, the observation round lasts for several months. The French talk of a "funny war," but the English call it a "phony war." Before the end of September, Poland is vanquished, crushed, dismembered. Meanwhile, France and England hop up and down to warm up.

Some Polish officers who escaped the disaster and fled

to France decide to form an army in exile. They hope to reconquer Poland, or at least to help their allies. All the Poles living in France must enroll in this army. Me, I don't feel so Polish anymore. Besides, I must take care of my family. I'm a young father. . . .

Cops ask me for my papers in the street. A young man not wearing an army uniform—this seems wrong to them. They keep me for three days in their police station, then send me to the Polish army. I wonder whether the exiled officers really want Jews to join their army. These Poles tell me to stay home and wait.

"We'll write to you. We'll need you when we march in the streets of Warsaw. . . ."

I should have gone with my brothers. They came up with a good scheme: they enrolled in the Foreign Legion. After fighting for France, they'll be allowed to become French citizens. They don't fight much, actually. The Germans knock France out in a few weeks in May and June 1940. The captain of Jacques's unit gives his men one last order.

"We'll soon be surrounded. Put civilian clothes on and save your skin!"

Jacques obeys his officer and comes home.

As for Albert, the Germans catch him with his whole regiment and send him to a prisoners' camp in Alsace. He convinces the commander of the camp that he is a skilled tailor who can cut a nice suit for him. The commander, whom he measures carefully, sets him up in a room, gives him cloth and thread, comes every day to check his work, tries the suit on, looks at himself in the mirror, and grins with pleasure. Albert writes to Paule that everything is fine. She jumps on a train and comes to the camp. The commander gives Albert a day off so he can see his sister. Albert and Paule take the train and flee to the Free Zone in the south of France. Albert knows someone in the city of Montauban, so they settle there. Albert's wife and daughter join them after a few weeks.

The Germans pound the streets of Paris with their heavy boots. I don't feel like going out for walks anymore. In November 1940, posters appear with instructions for the Jews: we're supposed to go to our neighborhood's police station and register. The posters threaten "severe punishment" for whoever tries to slip away. One thing we know about Germans: when they say "severe punishment," they mean it. It isn't as if I had a choice. With a name like Moszek, the Polish version of Moshe or Moses, I can hardly pretend I'm not Jewish. My mother, my brother Jacques, my friends at the club, everybody registers. The police employees write down our names and addresses, then stamp the word *Jew* on our residence cards.

Six months later, on May 12, 1941, I receive a summons by mail:

Prefecture of Police

Mr. Wisniak, Moszek Ajzyk will report in person, with a member of his family or a friend, on May 14,

> *1941 at 7.00 hours, 2, rue Japy (sports hall) for a review of his situation. ID papers will be requested. Any person failing to report on the designated day and hour may expect the most severe punishment.*

I know the Japy sports hall quite well. I boxed there! It is not far from our home, so I walk there with Rachel, after dropping Élie at my mother's. This summons is strange. Why should a family member come along?

Rachel worries.

"Maybe we should have found a way to join your brother and sister in Montauban."

"You'd leave your job? And what about me? Would I find new customers over there?"

As we come closer to rue Japy, we see other Polish Jews. Hundreds of people are gathered inside the sports hall. I find my brother Jacques and several of my friends from the club. The cops ask our wives or friends to go to our homes and bring back a suitcase with our clothes and our things, because they're sending us to a camp. So we know why someone had to come along. I see tears running down Jacques's face.

"My little Rosette was still sleeping. I didn't even say good-bye to her. . . ."

"As for me, I won't be at home for Élie's birthday: he's going to be two tomorrow. Rachel planned to bake a cake. She bought two little candles. I built a small wooden truck, with iron wheels. The bastards! They really fooled us. . . . If they had mentioned a suitcase, we wouldn't have come. We would have tried to hide, or we would have escaped to Montauban. What a clever trick: *come with someone* . . ."

"The Germans told the French police how it's done, I guess."

"You believe the French can't think up such a scheme? The police are the same everywhere!"

One hour later, Carole (Jacques's wife) and Rachel bring us our clothes. When we ask the cops where we're going, they answer, "A camp," but won't say more. Where is this camp? In France? In Germany? How long will we stay there? Rachel thought about that. She put a thick woolen sweater, my coat, and my winter boots in my backpack.

CHAPTER 8

A small town named Pithiviers

Here I am, carrying my backpack just like in the old camping days, boarding a bus with my brother Jacques and other Jews. I ask Rachel not to worry and to give Élie a kiss for me. She is comforting Carole, who is crying loudly.

Through the windows of the bus I see Parisians on the sidewalks. They are going to work or hurrying home. They worry about money or whatever. They should rejoice at being free! We cross the Seine River. I see the high towers and proud steeple of Notre Dame Cathedral. Although I've lived in Paris more than ten years, I've never visited Notre Dame. I promise myself I'll do it as soon as I'm free again. Yeah, and I'll climb to the top of the Eiffel Tower, too.

The bus joins a herd of others in the courtyard of the Austerlitz train station. My brother's face, which was very dark, lightens a little.

"We're staying in France. If we went to Germany, we would start from the *Gare de l'Est*."

We board a train very similar to the ones I used to take on weekends. Those were happy times! We go across quiet suburbs. I recognize the lazy bends of the Seine, then the Fontainebleau forest. Now we see fields and meadows. The train stops in a small town named Pithiviers. All the passengers feel relieved. Nothing bad can happen to us this close to Paris.

We discover the camp. . . . According to the military guards, it was built to house German prisoners at the beginning of the war, when France still hoped to win. It contains twenty wooden barracks with corrugated iron roofs, a dispensary, some offices. The barracks are on the spartan side. They've made two-tiered bunks with rough planks and covered them with straw. I think of the carters in our courtyard, who slept in the stables with their horses. . . . They give us very little food.

"In the German concentration camps," Jacques says, "they always keep the prisoners hungry. This breaks their will and their resistance."

At least the guards let us write to our wives, and soon our wives send us parcels full of food.

By and by, we learn what happened. They arrested 3,500 Polish Jews and a few dozen Czech Jews on May 14. They sent them to Pithiviers and to another town nearby, Beaune-la-Rolande. The official statement says they had to arrest foreign Jews, all of them parasites and illicit peddlers whom they would put to work.

Jacques finds it pretty funny.

"Before the war, all these anti-Semitic parties complained that the Jews took work from the Frenchmen. Now they tell us we're lazy parasites and they want to put us to work!"

"I'd like them to give us some work. Doing nothing all day makes me nervous."

"You know this camp is full of Jewish scholars? People who came to France to study science or medicine. I heard they're planning conferences."

"Go to your conferences. I just wish they'd give us a ball so we could play soccer."

In July, the camp's commander says our families will be allowed to visit us. Weeks before the day, I imagine the moment when I'll see my Rachel and my little Élie. Then this moment comes and it is over so fast. In two months, my son has changed. He speaks better, he has a new way of smiling. . . .

On June 21, 1941, the Germans attack the Soviet Union without any warning. In 1939, Stalin had signed a treaty with Hitler, because he wasn't ready for a war. I hope he is ready now. The German army won't reach Moscow as easily as Warsaw or Paris, so the war will last a long time. Maybe I'll stay years in this camp and my son will grow up far away from me.

The guards are looking for guys willing to work outside the camp. I go and fetch Jacques as fast as I can.

"Come, Jacques, this is a fantastic chance!"

"Yes, this will relieve us of this dreadful boredom."

"I mean a chance to escape. Once we're outside, it will be easy."

No luck. They separate us: they send Jacques to a Pithiviers workshop, me to a big farm with twenty comrades. As I've always lived in a city, I've never seen a peasant. I thought peasants were poor people, like factory workers, exploited and oppressed by the rich. Well, the peasant who owns this farm doesn't merely exploit us—he treats us like slaves. We must harvest, plow, make hay, tend the cattle. It's really tough. It never stops. He feeds us so little that we can hardly stand. He seems to resent having workers who cost him nothing. Instead of thanking us, he insults us.

"You rotten Jews, you're good for nothing. Stealing our money is easier than holding a scythe!"

The guard who takes us there has never seen such heartlessness.

"He treats you worse than dogs!"

This guard is a good guy. I wouldn't say the same about his colleagues, far from it. He doesn't think it's right that we're being kept in a camp.

"Listen, fellows. When I take you to the farm, I can't watch you all. If I notice that one or two are missing when we get there, what can I do about it? I can't leave the prisoners and go warn the other guards, so I have to wait until evening to report it."

Obviously, he is telling us we should escape. I talk to my brother.

"It is simple. We hide in the woods, then we walk all night heading south. We cross the line that separates the Occupied Zone from the Free Zone. You know where Montauban is?"

"Somewhere near Toulouse, I think."

"We'll ask people. We'll get there eventually, one way or another."

"Okay, but I can't leave my workshop. We're just six Jews with one guard. He keeps his eyes on us. Why don't you go by yourself? I'll follow when I can."

I could escape by myself, that's true. But what about Jacques? Without me, will he be able to shake off the guards, hide, reach the other side of France? He is so sluggish, sometimes. . . . Even in the camp, he finds books and spends time reading and dreaming like a student. Becoming an outlaw isn't something you learn in books. I can't leave him behind. I must take care of him.

CHAPTER 9

These cars usually carry cattle

I didn't take my chance when I should have and now it's too late. More than a hundred prisoners escaped during the first six months. They say the Germans are furious. The guards put up more barbed wire around the camp. Nobody goes outside to work anymore. We hear rumors that they'll empty the camp. From May 1942 on, hundreds of men leave every week. We don't know where they go. Some guards talk about a camp in Compiègne, others say Drancy, near Paris. More sinister rumors mention camps in Germany or in the Ukraine. Lacking definite information, we make up a name, *Pitchipoï*, to name this mysterious location in Eastern Europe where they deport Jews.

My brother goes in June. I leave on July 17. On the way to the Pithiviers train station, I walk with Brod, whom I've known a long time. He is a tailor. My other brother, Albert, worked in his workshop when we came to France. He boxed for a year or two, on and off, then stopped because he found it too tiring. He is a placid man, always ready to smile. I used to see him also on the banks of the Marne River. He's lucky—in Pithiviers, he worked in the kitchen.

"Say, Brod, you look good! While everybody was hungry, you were gaining weight."

"Come on, Wisniak, you're not that thin yourself!"

"My wife sent me food. I did get fatter when I stopped boxing. I went from a hundred and eight pounds to a hundred and eighty-five! I tried to keep in shape, though. I exercised on weekends."

"I remember. You were always swimming and playing volleyball. How's Rachel?"

"Last time I saw her, she was fine. We have a son, Élie. He's three years old. What about your children?"

"I have one more."

"Four?"

"I like large families. I have eight brothers and sisters. My last one, actually, I've hardly even seen her. This jacket you're wearing is nice. Did your brother cut it?"

"Of course, Albert did it."

"He's a fine craftsman. When he started working by himself, I lost my best worker. Did he marry?"

"He married just before the war. He has a daughter."

"You know what? Maybe they're going to take us back to Paris and free us for Bastille Day, on July 14. We'll be able to dance with our wives!"

"I don't think the Germans will let the French celebrate Bastille Day. My brother told me France isn't even a republic anymore. If I'd known, I would have gone to America."

"If I'd known, I wouldn't have registered as a Jew. They can't control everybody. Do you know the story of the two Jews taking a walk in Moscow?"

"No."

"This was in the times of the czar. One of the Jews only has a residence permit. Suddenly, a cop comes at them. 'Start running,' says the permitless one to the other. 'The cop will run after you, but you don't have to worry, since you have a permit. In the meantime, I'll escape.' The Jew begins to run. The cop runs after him and catches him after a while. 'Well, well, you bum, you don't have a permit?' The Jew is out of breath. He shows his permit: 'Pardon me . . . Your honor . . . I do have a permit . . .' The cop stares at him. 'But then, why did you run away?' 'My doctor told me this was good for my health.' The cop is panting, too. 'Didn't you see I was running after you?' 'Of course I did. I thought your doctor had given you the same advice!' "

In the Pithiviers station, a long freight train is waiting for us. Brod shows me a tiny latticed window above the cars' door.

"These are cattle cars."

"You mean these cars usually carry cattle to the slaughterhouse? This isn't a good omen."

The guards deliver us to German soldiers. They cram

eighty men into every car. I've often taken the Paris subway at rush hour. There were so many passengers that I could hardly breathe. When I couldn't stand it anymore, I would step out at a station and wait for the next train. Every time it happened, I swore I'd be more careful in the future and avoid rush hour. Well, I haven't been careful enough. I'm standing in a train car at rush hour, except I can't step out. The train rolls on during the day and until the end of the night, then it stops. Brod lifts me up so I can look through the grilled opening.

"We're in a station. I can't see the name of the city, but the people are speaking German. The bastards!"

"What is it?"

"They're laughing at me. Wait, one of the soldiers is coming in this direction. Does anyone speak German well here?"

Most of us know Yiddish, which is very close to German, but one of us, an Austrian Jew, also speaks real German. He asks the soldier whether we could empty the bucket that serves as a toilet bowl for eighty men and have a little water. We've had nothing to drink for twenty-four hours. The heat of eighty feverish bodies adds several degrees to the summer temperature. The soldier, after asking an officer's permission, lets the Austrian Jew out. Four comrades have bottles in their bags. The Austrian guy finds a tap and fills up the bottles. Four quarts of water for eighty thirsty throats. One sip each.

The train starts again. Hours follow hours. Hotter and hotter. No food since yesterday. One sip to drink. Some men moan, lose their minds, and shriek like beasts. How long will I be able to hold on before I start to shriek, too? The train slows down. Stops again. Where are the soldiers? From all the cars we hear shouts in French, Yiddish, German.

"We're thirsty!"

"Men are sick!"

"Bucket overflowing!"

Men wearing black uniforms walk alongside the train. They're SS, special police. It seems they have replaced the soldiers.

"Stop this racket, you Jewish pigs, otherwise we'll shoot."

To show they mean business, they do shoot with a machine gun inside one of the cars. Nobody shouts anymore. A dreadful silence falls on the train like a slab of lead. Pithiviers was no fun, but we're beginning to understand that we'll soon remember it as paradise lost. We're heading toward unspeakable horrors.

When I was a child, hunger was my faithful companion. I never knew thirst, however. I'm discovering this cruel sensation now. I can't think about anything else. My throat is as raspy as sandpaper. My tongue is twisting inside my mouth, looking for a few drops of spittle. My lips are burning. The others groan, rave, scream: "I don't want to die!" We muffle their screams with shirts, lest the SS shoot into our car at the next stop. Some faint but stay upright, held up by the closeness of their neighbors. Others slide to the floor, unconscious or maybe dead. Is this how they had imagined their death? From thirst and exhaustion in a cattle car . . . ?

The bucket overflowed long ago. A frightful, nauseating stink permeates the car. When we stop in a station, the SS shout, "You stinking Jews! You're just shit!"

We move in turn near the opening to breathe some fresh air. I see Brod in the distance. He smiles at me. He's still alive.

My thoughts seem to slow down. At times, I fall asleep standing up. When my mind clears somewhat, I tell myself that this trip has to end sooner or later. I'll leave this car, dead or alive.

CHAPTER 10

Did you see the name on the signs? Auschwitz

Toward the end of the third night, as the sliver of sky we see through the grated slit turns gray, the train stops and we hear shouting:

"*Aussteigen! Los! Los!* (Get out! Come on! Come on!)"

We're there.

The SS open the car's door. They order us to leave our bags inside.

"We'll bring them to you later."

We know it's not true. We're a thousand guys in the train and our bags aren't even marked. How would we find them? During this trip, exhaustion froze our thoughts, but we knew one thing: we were traveling toward death. Our material goods lost any value. So I'll never see my faithful backpack again. What do I care about pajamas and a toothbrush? If only I can hold on to my life. . . .

After three days in the gloom of the cattle car, the morning light dazzles me. The train has stopped along a kind of low platform. I can't see it too well. My legs are stiff. In spite of all this, I jump down, I hurry, I run. The SS are hitting us with long rubbery clubs to get us moving. Ouch! This hurts like hell. While I'm rubbing my shoulder, I notice there is a steel ball at the end of the club. Some comrades fall down, knocked senseless.

This station is in the middle of nowhere. SS guards armed with rifles, holding German shepherds on leashes, stand every five feet on the platform. Suddenly, one of these SS starts shouting. The German language may not sound as musical as Yiddish; it is nevertheless quite beautiful in the poems by Goethe or Schiller. The SS seem to use another language, a shouted or barked one. What does he say? We try to see what's happening. Something's wrong with a comrade in the next car. Although he left his suitcase behind, he kept a small parcel under his arm. Three SS knock him down with the butt of their rifles.

"We told you to leave everything behind!"

They break his skull with the rifles. One of the guards jumps aside deftly, like a boxer, to avoid dirtying his shiny black boots with blood and brains.

We were talking in low voices: "Did you see the name on the signs? Auschwitz."

"It's a German name. Do you think we're in Germany?"

The death of our comrade makes us fall silent. I don't feel thirst, hunger, exhaustion anymore. Although I haven't slept for three nights, I am wide awake.

I try to remember whether I have ever seen a cold-blooded

murder like this one. The carters in our courtyard. Knives, gunshots. Mazik's stray bullets. "Don't go near the window," my mother said. I'm surrounded by killers and I can't hide.

An SS officer makes an announcement.

"There are trucks over there for those of you who are tired or ill. The other ones must walk to the camp."

I don't like these trucks. They let us die of thirst in the train, they shot at random inside a car with their machine guns, they just killed one of us for no valid reason. This sudden kindness toward tired and sick Jews doesn't sound right to me. Since they kill Jews so easily, I bet these trucks won't drive them to a nice rest home.

We walk in rows of five toward the camp. The SS kill one comrade with their rifle butts because he's dragging his feet and stumbling, another because he vomits. Brod walks next to me.

"They'll kill us all," he whispers.

"Maybe they only want to scare us."

"If so, they're succeeding quite well."

They kill another guy just because he is talking. After discovering thirst on the train, I discover fear. I won't pretend I've never been afraid, but it was always a feeling I could control. All I had to do was raise my fists and fight. The fear that overwhelms me as we are coming near the camp's gate is of a different kind. It is new to me—dreadful, ghastly. For the first time in my life, I feel unable to fight back. I am ready to accept my fate.

A sentence is written in cast iron above the gate: "*Arbeit macht frei* (Work makes you free)." We stop before walking in. An SS points toward the maxim: "If one of you is too tired to work, let him come forward."

We understand that our life is not worth much in this strange place, which we used to call Pitchipoï before we knew its real name was Auschwitz. Anyone who comes forward will be clubbed to death.

The SS smiles.

"All volunteering for work, I see. . . ."

The SS stay outside the gate. We enter the camp, where we see some brick houses and rows of barracks similar to the ones in Pithiviers. Men carrying clubs take charge of us. They drive us into the first barrack and order us to remove our clothes. A prisoner shaves a wide stripe on top of our head with a barber's clippers. Two other ones shave all the hair on our bodies. Their clippers are blunt, they hurry, so they tear off great patches of skin under our arms and between our legs. Then someone tattoos a number on our left forearm. I cease to be Moshe or Maurice Wisniak and become 48950: *Achtundvierzigtausend neunhundertfünfzig*.

The tattoo guy is the first one who speaks to me (in Yiddish).

"Have you got gold or diamonds?"

"Of course not."

"A pity. It could have lengthened your life. You have three weeks left, more or less. If you're still alive after three weeks, then perhaps you'll last a few more. Especially if you find a quiet job, like me. Where do you come from?"

"France."

"Are you French?"

"No, Polish."

"Did they catch many Jews in France?"

"Thousands. Tell me, where are we?"

"You haven't figured it out yet? We're in hell!"

"I mean, where is Auschwitz? In Germany?"

"This side of the camp is called Birkenau. We're somewhere south of Cracow. Actually, Auschwitz and Birkenau are German names for Ozwiecim and Brzezinka,* a town and village of ours."

"So we're in Poland? I was pretty sure I would never see the country of my birth again. . . ."

"You were born in Poland. You'll die in Poland."

The shaved stripe on our skull makes it easy to recognize us in case we try to escape. This is rather unlikely, but still, to be on the safe side, they paint two large letters with white paint on the back of our jackets: KZ, which stand for *Konzentrationslager*. They give us a kind of gray cap, but otherwise we keep our regular clothes. Because of the heat in the car, I have taken off my winter coat. It's gone forever now, along with my backpack. I'm wearing the jacket that Albert made for me. I hope Rachel and Élie are safe in Montauban with

---

*Pronounced Osviaitsim and Bzhaisinka.

him. I think about my other brother, Jacques, who left three weeks before me. If it is true that few prisoners survive for more than three weeks, then I'll have to accept the idea that my elder brother is already dead.

The men with the clubs order us to stand outside in rows of five. They shout exactly like SS. We walk across the camp, when suddenly, I see—Is this possible? Walking corpses! Two corpses are carrying a third one. . . . I have always considered myself a tough guy. I didn't shake when the SS murdered comrades on the platform. I used to see blue cadavers on the bridge across the Vistula, while I was gliding from stove to stove. But walking corpses? They move slowly, as if they were climbing a mountain, as if they wanted to save whatever strength they retain. All of a sudden, in the middle of July, I feel so cold I begin to shiver. I try not to look at their emaciated faces, their bulging eyes, the grin that uncovers their teeth.

Our guides are grinning, too.

"In one month, you'll be like them, shitbags. If you're lucky enough to be alive in one month!"

They take us to the eighth barrack. We don't call it a barrack but a *block*. The men with clubs are *kapos*.* Among the prisoners, there are Jews from Poland who understand the German language, but also Jews from France and Holland who don't, as well as ordinary Poles or Russian war prisoners

---

*For *Kameraden Polizei*.

who aren't even Jewish. If they want to stay alive, they'd better learn German pretty fast. Everybody knows at least kapo, block, and also *Lager* (the camp), *Häftling* (a prisoner), *Mütze* (the cap), and, of course, *Drecksack* (shitbag), *Dreckfresser* (shit eater), *Scheissjude* (shitty Jew), *Schweinehund* (pig dog), and *Hirenzine* (son of a bitch, a Yiddish insult that even the Germans use).

In Pithiviers, they crammed a hundred of us in barracks that were built for fifty. In Auschwitz, our whole train enters block eight. Close to a thousand men! The guy in charge of the block or *Blockältester** (block senior) is a non-Jewish Pole named Marek. He starts counting us, with the help of a dozen assistants. At the same time, his deputy, the *Stubendienst* (room servant), a Jewish Pole, begins a speech in Yiddish.

"My name is Laybich. Listen to me, you Hirenzine. I'd rather kill you all than break one of my nails. You think you're wise guys, right? While I was stuck in Poland, you lived like princes in France. You drank champagne, you spent your money on French whores. Well, that's over, my friends. The strongest of you will live three weeks. In one month, you'll all be dead and other Hirenzine will come and replace you. We're all going to die, but I'll be the last to kick in."

He goes on and on with his speech, half-rambling, half-spitting the vilest abuse. A well-dressed and rather stiff

---

*This is probably a Yiddishism. In proper German, it would be *Blockälteste*.

Frenchman, an army officer perhaps, tries to ask a question, searching awkwardly for the right Yiddish words.

"I can't answer you now," Laybich says. "I'll take care of you later."

When his speech is over, he adds:

"You have eyes to see and ears to hear and a mouth full of shit that you'd better keep closed. You there, you interrupted me. Maybe you think this is some kind of a meeting. You'll see. . . ."

As the block senior hasn't finished counting us yet, the deputy walks in our midst and asks whether any of us has already killed, taken part in a burglary or armed robbery, spent time in jail.

"Come on, Hirenzine, don't be shy. Come and speak in the hollow of my ear!"

Several men approach him. We understand he is recruiting assistants for himself and for his boss. After a while, the block senior and his men have counted us all. The block senior doesn't speak Yiddish, only bad German.

"You too many. We plus you, one thousand and five. Not there room enough in block. One thousand only. You, you and also you and you, too old. Too much suffer here. I save you suffering. And you, talk too much."

He designates four prisoners, as well as the French officer. Right in front of us, his assistants beat them to death with their clubs, then line up the corpses outside the block.

The assistants bring in hundreds of rusty chamber pots

full of a brown liquid that they call "coffee." Where did they find all these chamber pots? Five men to a pot, they say. Brod, three comrades, and I, we try to control our thirst and take turns drinking quietly. In other groups, there are conflicts and shouting. Laybich writes down the numbers of the noisiest drinkers.

"I like quiet," he says. "Those who disturb the peace will be lined up tomorrow morning in front of the block, like these five."

We hope he is joking, but nobody feels like laughing.

Toward the end of the day, several thousand prisoners come back from outside the camp, where they work in groups called *Kommandos*. We recognize comrades who left Pithivers one or two weeks before us. They give us some advice.

"You've just arrived, but you must understand all the laws of the camp before tomorrow. He who understands in twenty-four hours is twice more likely to survive than he who needs forty-eight hours."

"Beware the *Bindenträgern* (men with armbands). They belong to the staff. Their assignment is written on the band: blockältester, stubendienst, kapo. They're former German or Polish criminals, Jewish thieves, or prisoners who choose to become killers to escape death for a while. We call them barons.* Try not to offend them if you want to stay alive."

---

*The German word used was *Prominenten*, or important persons.

"Keep your shoes on at night. If you take them off, you're dead. Either someone steals them, or your feet swell and you can't put them on again. Then you must use the camp's wooden clogs. After two or three days, your feet are so bruised that you can't walk anymore. You limp behind the others when going to work, so the kapo gets rid of you."

A guy I knew before the war says something I don't understand: "You're lucky. They could have gassed you."

CHAPTER 11

It seems to me he is heavier than a living man

I spend my first night in the camp. Two tiers of six-foot-wide planks run along the wall. We sleep with our feet toward the wall and our heads near the central passage, lying on our side, stacked like forks in a cutlery drawer. I am glad to lie down for the first time since we left Pithiviers. I'd be able to sleep much better if I took off my heavy boots, but that's impossible. "If you take off your boots, you're dead." Now and then, all the stacked bodies turn over together to change sides, without waking up.

Just after I close my eyes, I hear beatings, screams, and the deputy shouting.

"*Aufstehen! Aufstehen!* (Get up!) Up with you, Hirenzine! Out! Faster, faster!"

The morning has come already. . . . I jump down from my bunk and run outside. I receive only one small blow on the way. A French Jew, who slept on the same plank as me, receives a shower of blows while he's putting on his shoes.

His face is covered with blood. He has delicate hands and the look of an intellectual worker. I think about my older brother. . . .

Whereas five bodies were lined up in front of the block last night, we now discover thirty, set in groups of five, naked, with tattooed arms sticking out so the number is easy to read. Laybich the deputy delivers a short eulogy for them.

"I gave them coffee, but they weren't satisfied. Let this be a lesson to you, my friends!"

"What did he say?" the French Jew asks me in a whisper. "I don't understand Yiddish, you know. Can you translate?"

"Shut up, or we'll end up the same way!"

It is four A.M. or so. We stand up in rows of five until eight. Marek and Laybich call our numbers, count us again and again. Marek the block senior orders:

"*Mützen ab! Mützen auf!*" (Caps off! Caps on!)

This Marek probably dreamed of leading an orchestra when he was a kid. He wants our thousand caps to slap our thousand thighs together. *Mützen ab! Mützen auf!* Ten times. A hundred times. One hour. Two hours. We improve our act pretty fast when Marek kills five of us whose rhythm was slightly off.

At eight, an SS inspects us and counts the dead. After he's gone, we drink our morning "coffee," then go look for a kommando. There is a kind of work pickup in the middle of the camp. The old-timers warn us.

"During the first few days, you won't be able to find a

kommando outside the camp. The kapos prefer to pick up men they already know. Don't worry and just wait. So many die that you'll get a job soon."

In the meantime, we work inside the camp. I find work in the undertakers' kommando. We carry away the bodies lined up in front of the blocks. I'm a strong and healthy newcomer. I don't look like the living skeletons who frightened me so much yesterday. The kapo decides I can carry a corpse all by myself. I hold his legs over my shoulder, like suspenders. He hangs down my back. His head bumps on my calves at every step. His hands drag on the ground. It seems to me he is heavier than a living man.

We carry the bodies to the *Totenkammer* (the chamber of the dead), where a kommando of dentists under the supervision of an SS pulls out gold teeth. If someone doesn't unload his corpse head first, mouth opened, the SS has him killed right away. This produces a new corpse, whom nobody had to carry—he walked to the Totenkammer on his own two feet. The SS is always angry because bodies come in with their gold teeth missing. Some prisoners sell theirs for a piece of bread. What's more, the block senior and the kapos will look inside your mouth, hoping to see something shiny down there. Some pull out your gold teeth without killing you, others kill you first. I'm lucky! I was always too poor to buy gold teeth.

I'll go crazy if I have to keep carrying corpses. I'm ready to try the worst outside kommandos—the ones the old-timers tell us to avoid because their kapos are ferocious killers. On the third day, I try a digging kommando. We're removing small hillocks in order to flatten a field where they intend to build a factory or something. The old-timers were right—the kapo and his assistants the *Vorarbeiter* (foremen) are murderers. They kill fifteen prisoners out of two hundred. They order us to bring back the bodies, so I end up with two legs on my shoulders and a head bumping against my calves, like yesterday.

I change to another kommando. I work in a swamp, which we have to fill up with stones and garbage. Something very unusual happens here. Just as a kapo is going to beat a tall newcomer with his club, the guy grabs the club and hits the kapo. This is a terrible scandal, because the kapo is a German criminal. Nobody is supposed to pull one hair off a German's head! All the kapos and foremen come at once to their colleague's rescue, but the tall prisoner is fighting like a devil. He is a young, strong athlete, used to fighting and winning.

The SS who stand guard over us think the whole mess is quite funny. The kapos call them for help: "Shoot him!"

"Go get him yourselves, you cowards! Shitbags!"

The tall man defies the kapos:

"You won't kill me with your clubs. You'll have to shoot me!"

At least twelve kapos and foremen attack him together. He fights back bravely, but can't resist for very long. In the end, they drown him in the swamp. When it's over, the bastards take their revenge on us. None of the six hundred prisoners in the kommando is spared, and our tormentors kill fifty prisoners. All the other ones are injured or bruised to various degrees.

I ask the old-timers for advice.

"Is there a safer job?"

"It's the same thing everywhere," they say.

I try digging again. More men are killed or wounded than are spared. We can't carry them back to the camp, so the kapos have to send for trucks.

At the end of the first week, out of one thousand prisoners on my train, five hundred are still alive. We're all very weak. In the morning, we drink the blackish liquid called coffee. When we come back from work, we drink another liquid, called soup. Pieces of turnip hide at the bottom of the huge pot. The block senior keeps them for himself and his good friends. Brod and I, we're lucky: we have some spare fat on our body. Many prisoners lose weight very fast. In the camp's slang, the walking corpses, the fleshless skeletons covered by a thin layer of skin, are called Muselman.* As they can't climb up onto the bunks, they sleep on the

---

*Nobody knows why a dying person was called a Muselman—Yiddish for Moslem. Some say that the word actually stood for "fakir," meaning a very thin person. I've also read that a great famine affected the Moslem province of Bengal (today's Bangladesh) in the early 1940s. Three million people died of hunger. Maybe someone first used the word after seeing pictures of skin-and-bone Bengali Moslems.

ground, under the lower bunk, in mire and filth. They suffer from diarrhea, but don't have enough strength to go empty their bowels outside.

The French Jew with the delicate hands who slept on my bunk died a long time ago. He told me he worked in a couture workshop in Paris. He used to take off his fine Italian shoes to sleep, so they vanished on the second night. A kapo probably killed him outside, then his kommando brought him directly to the Totenkammer.

All the kapos and foremen drool when they see my heavy winter boots. They force me to take them off so they can swap with me. My feet are like Cinderella's. The boots are always too small for them! To be on the safe side, I decorate them with iron wire, so it looks like the sole is going to separate from the upper part and they leave me alone.

I stay alive. I spend hours on my feet when Marek counts us and recounts us. Every evening, Laybich the deputy forces us to squat like frogs, legs apart. He writes down the number of those who can't maintain a straight back. I stay motionless for three hours, four hours.

Laybich and his death angels roam through the block in the middle of the night. They pull from their bunks the men who must cease to live and strangle them noiselessly. In the morning, we discover twenty bodies, or twenty-five, lined up in front of the block. The SS who inspects the blocks at eight a.m. finds it more convenient to count the bodies in fives. A ghost of a smile appears on his face when he sees a lot of corpses. Auschwitz is a factory for producing corpses.

I'm sure the SS on the watchtowers also like to count the corpses, to alleviate their boredom. What do the bodies resemble from up there? Matches? No, they're not far enough away. Bundles of firewood, maybe. When they count the bodies, the SS call them *Stücke*, which means pieces. The watchtower guards count the pieces in front of the blocks. Five pieces, ten, fifteen, twenty, twenty-five pieces . . .

Sometimes, a comrade dies of exhaustion at three A.M., after Laybich and his angels have completed their round. Then, when Marek counts us, he comes up one short. He sends people to look inside the block. They find our comrade's lifeless body in a dark corner.

Marek gets mad at us.

"I had twenty-five and now look what you've done, you Hirenzine!"

The SS wants a multiple of five, so Marek kills four more of us to have his thirty pieces.

CHAPTER 12

I am not allowed to hit a German

I work in yet another digging kommando with my friend Brod. Three young SS drive by in a car. They pass by slowly, twice, as if they were looking for something, then stop in front of me.

"You, Jew! You seem strong."

"You know how to fight, I bet."

"We'll find an opponent for you."

They want to have some fun. They're twenty years old. They're like children—we're their toys. They pick a prisoner who is much taller than me, but has already become a Muselman. They think the contrast between a tough midget and a gaunt giant is entertaining.

Many kapos and foremen have spent time in jail before coming to the camp. They were thieves, hoodlums. The stronger among them feel a kind of sadistic pleasure in killing a poor Muselman with a single blow. These two SS want to know whether I can do it. It is a kind of entrance exam. The other prisoners go on working. They watch out of the corner of their eyes.

I throw big, hard punches, but I hold them back at the last fraction of a second so that I don't hit him too hard. The Muselman's bulging eyes look at me without seeing anything. He doesn't care. He doesn't try to fight. He's like a shadow, actually. If this goes on, I'm afraid I'll start crying. The two SS are not satisfied.

"What kind of joke is this?"

"*Schweinkopf!* (Pig's head!) You're making fun of us!"

"If you don't know what a real punch is like, I'll show you. Come here. Look at me. Follow my eyes!"

The SS looks to the right. I follow his eyes. Immediately, I get punched on the right side. Now he looks left. I expect a hook on the left, but he hits on the right again and laughs. This guy is more than just a fighter: he's a real boxer. The SS tend to prefer boxing to golf or tennis. I played these kinds of games, at the club, to train my reflexes. If I could hit back, the game would become more interesting. Yeah, but I can't hit a German. Assaulting a member of the superior race is a crime punishable by death. He hits me right and left, to the head, to the stomach, for a good thirty minutes. My abdominal muscles haven't melted away yet, so I tighten them as much as I can. My face is bloody, but at least I avoid dying of a burst liver. He notices that I'm trying to dodge his blows. He sneers, and then hits harder, as if I were a punching bag.

I'm beginning to feel groggy. I guess I'll drift into death without being aware of it. This is not an unpleasant idea. I hear vaguely that the two other SS are interfering.

"Leave him alone."

"He's a good boxer. Maybe we can convince him to fight."

They ask four prisoners to carry me to the barrack they use as a kitchen. They lock me inside a wooden box full of knives and forks. I am conscious but unable to react, like in a dream. The box is three feet long, one and a half feet wide, one and a half feet high. It is similar to a child's coffin.

"Close the lid," the SS say.

"Roll the box on the ground."

"Faster. Come on! Faster, you shitbags!"

The prisoners roll the box for maybe hundreds of feet. Strangely, I find this punishment rather restful. I am crammed so tight in the box that the knives and forks have no room to fly around and hurt me. What (and whom) is this cutlery for? While we eat with our fingers from chamber pots, there are boxes full of knives and forks in the kitchen! Our masters probably eat on embroidered tablecloths, on fine china. It is said that Dutch Jews bring enormous amounts of food in their luggage: preserves, rice, dried fruit. I wonder what kind of fruit grows in Holland. When I came to Paris, I ate oranges and bananas for the first time in my life, and even African figs and dates. . . . The French guards hooked two cars full of food to the back of our train when we left Pithiviers—for us to eat on our trip.

I remember that one of these intellectual Jews who had come to France to study medicine tried to protest while we were waiting in a station: "Give us food! Open the supply cars!"

"Shut up. What they'll give you is a burst of bullets."

He wanted to write a letter of complaint: "We'll all sign it. We'll give it to the commander of the camp."

Another medical student sighed. "The Nazis began persecuting the Jews in 1933, nearly ten years ago. You know how the Jews defended themselves? They wrote hundreds of petitions, in Europe and even in America. Look what it did for us!"

All these students are already dead. *Arbeit macht frei*. They're free, now.

One of the guys rolling the box whispers to me that I should try to scream, to please the SS. I wonder whether I'll follow his advice. I'd rather go on floating in my dreamlike state. Besides, I don't have enough strength left to scream. I can't emit any sound. . . . And then, something inside me decides that I want to live, after all. I utter a kind of hoarse whine that soon turns into a scream. How long do I roll with the knives and forks? I don't know. The men stop moving the box. They open the lid.

I hear Polish kapos.

"Incredible. He's still alive."

"He'll die now. A pity, too—he was a brave one."

"Water!"

Who shouted "Water"? I think it is the man who was inside the box. Through a reddish mist, I see an amazing event: a kapo brings me a cup of water! Someone sticks toilet paper on my face as a dressing for my wounds. My comrades hold me during the walk back to the camp. I hear the kapos talking to the guards.

"We have twenty dead and one hurt."

Usually, they take the wounded to block seven, a kind of hospital without doctors where the only cure is death. They spare me because I'm a hero: the Jew who refuses to kill a Muselman and resists the SS.

Brod says I was wrong to risk my life.

"That was a close call. You could have died. If you had hit the Muselman a little harder, you would have put a stop to his pain. He's one or two days away from the end. It wouldn't make such a big difference."

"No difference for him, maybe, but for me, yes. I have a little boy, you know. What will I tell him when I come back? I don't want his father to be a murderer."

In the following days, even the most ferocious kapos treat me with respect. They give me easy tasks. I work like an automaton. The SS punched my head so many times that I can't seem to regain my full mind.

"He's finished," my comrades say when they look at me. "He's good for block seven."

I kind of envy a Muselman who runs toward the electric fence to end it all. The comrades say I'm brave, but this man is braver than me. The watchtower guard kills him with two rifle shots. A Muselman will never reach the barbed wire. How could he run fast enough? And just in case the guard were to miss him, foremen armed with clubs patrol the fence. Their job is to catch the suicide runners and kill them slowly. It is simpler than repairing the fence after an electric short circuit.

All the prisoners run to cover when the watchtower guard starts shooting. They're afraid the guard might try to hit a few more targets just for fun. Me, I stay there like a fool, oblivious to the din around me. A kapo orders me to bring the corpse to the Totenkammer. Once more, I carry a bloody body on my back.

CHAPTER 13

Who is this stranger who saves my life?

I live in a permanent daze. I don't even recognize my comrades anymore. Brod holds my hand as if I were a child and takes me to a good kommando, meaning a kommando where the kapo doesn't kill his workers. We pull a large cart full of boxes and barrels from one camp to the other. There are two camps: Auschwitz I and II. The second one is also called Birkenau. That's where I live, or rather, survive. We pull the cart two miles in one direction, then two miles in the other direction, all day long. I run to the front to help my comrades pull the cart and to the back to help push it. I help them raise the cart when it's stuck in mud. I load and unload barrels weighing one hundred pounds.

Actually, I don't know I'm doing all this. Brod tells me about it later.

"You worked twice as hard as anybody else!"

Most prisoners suffer from diarrhea. We find it very

difficult to stay clean. Standing for hours while the block senior counts us is terribly painful. I may still be strong enough to carry barrels, but my willpower has become so weak that I let the contents of my bowels run down my legs. If only we could wash. . . . Laybich the deputy hates people who stink. After the morning call, he comes to me, pinching his nose with two fingers:

"You've lived long enough. I'll take care of you."

He writes my number in his notebook. So that's it. Over and done with. I passed the fateful three-week mark, but I'll die anyway. I'm getting ready to live my last day on earth, to see the sun for the last time. Tonight Laybich will kill me and line up my corpse with four others outside the block. I never knew my father and now my little Élie will not know his, either. I don't resist. I don't care. I'll join my kommando and work, like any other day. My kommando? Which one? Where am I? Utterly bewildered, I stop and look. I am inside the camp, a few steps away from the gate, alone. I could run toward the barbed wire. . . . If I'm lucky, the watchtower guard will kill me with a single shot to the head. Or the fence foremen will catch me and torture me. . . .

Suddenly, a voice shouts in German behind me: "You Schweinkopf! Stinking Frenchman! What are you doing here?"

Then the voice whispers in French: "Don't move. Someone is coming for you."

I don't understand what's happening. When I turn

around, there is no one behind me. All I see is a kapo walking away in the distance.

Who is this stranger who saves my life? In Paris, I knew several German Communists who had fled their country. Is he one of them? The camp is not ruled by reason but by madness; maybe my savior mistook me for someone else. In any case, he is a powerful man, a chief kapo or maybe even the *Lagerältester*, boss of all the block seniors. Two Polish kapos ask me to follow them.

They grumble, unaware that I understand their language: "Why does he want to save this Jew? It makes no sense."

"Stinks worse than a dog's ass!"

More than a month after my arrival in Auschwitz, I take my first shower. They throw away my jacket, a memento of my brother Albert, as well as all my other clothes, or rather, rags. I receive new clothes. My mysterious patron has sent me to the *Kleidenkammer* (clothes chamber) kommando, where privileged prisoners sort the clothes left on the trains. No wonder they gave me new clothes! We unstitch the yellow stars, look for hidden diamonds in the linings, then stack the pants, shirts, and jackets in packs of ten. The great German Reich will distribute these clothes to its poorest citizens in the name of *Winterhilfswerk* (winter help).

What's amazing is that we drink as much "coffee" as we want and eat solid food. My new comrades give me some advice.

"You should exchange your food for some charcoal. It will cure your diarrhea."

Every evening, we undress before we leave. The kapos check that we're not hiding jewels or gemstones. A kommando before us couldn't resist temptation. They were wiped out entirely.

Back in the block, Brod makes fun of my new jacket.

"You shouldn't have taken it. They fooled you! Either shorten the sleeves, or lengthen your arms. . . ."

"The old one, my brother had cut it."

"I know. You told me a million times. Hey, do you know the story of the Jew who goes to the tailor's?"

"Even if I know it, I never remember stories."

"He brings a piece of fabric and asks the tailor whether there is enough for a suit. The tailor looks at the piece, looks at the Jew. . . . 'You need more cloth,' he says. The Jew doesn't give up and goes to another tailor. 'Do I have enough cloth for a suit?' The tailor measures the piece, looks at the Jew. . . . 'Fine. I'll measure you. The suit will be ready on Monday.' When the Jew comes for his suit, he is amazed because the tailor's son, a five-year-old tot, wears a suit made of the same fabric. 'You succeeded in cutting a suit for me and one for your son. How come your colleague across the street told me I didn't have enough cloth?' 'Oh, the fellow across the street? He has two sons!' "

At first, we unstitch and stack men's shirts and jackets. Then we see silk blouses, skirts, dresses, scarves with Paris labels. They've started deporting our women. One day, we pull children's clothes out of a suitcase. Short pants, a vest knitted with love, tiny socks, a woolen cap for winter. Our faces darken. Every one of us thinks about his children, his little brothers and sisters, the future of the Jewish people.

They've already caught many women and children in Slovakia or somewhere. The parents who travel with small children bring chamber pots. That's where our coffee pots come from.

Having heard that some big shot is looking out for me, Laybich removes my number from his list. He treats me like a friend.

"You know, Wisniak, now that you wear such beautiful clothes, you can't sleep on a board with six lousy shitbags. Come here."

I can hardly believe my own ears. He calls me Wisniak instead of Hirenzine! He shows me a straw mattress, which I'll share with just one comrade. I sleep like a log. After a few days, I am a new man. The diarrhea is gone. I eat and get back some of my strength.

I come out of my daze. Until now, hopelessness, hunger, and primarily thirst have gripped my mind day and night. My thoughts never traveled beyond the barbed wire. Being able to drink as much as I want revives me. By and by, I begin to wonder and worry about what's going on outside the camp. Trainloads of Jews are arriving from Paris and bring news.

"Are they arresting women and children in France, now?"

"When did you leave?"

"The train left Pithiviers on July 17."

"So you haven't heard of the Vél d'Hiv* roundup?"

"Well, no."

"It happened the day before you left. They arrested everybody."

"But why women and children? They pretended they wanted to put the Jews to work."

"They had to, because they couldn't fill up their trains. In the beginning, they took only Polish Jews, men aged sixteen to forty."

"Yes. That's the way it was when they arrested me."

"Later they arrested younger and older guys, and also French Jews."

"This I know, too. There were French Jews on my train."

"It wasn't enough, so on July 16 they tried to catch as many people as they could. Men they deported right away, and also single women. Mothers and children they kept in the Vél d'Hiv, then in the Pithiviers camp. Do you know what? The bloody French went above and beyond the requests of the Germans, who had never asked for children."

"It didn't break the Germans' hearts, I'm sure."

"Of course. But they did need Berlin's approval to send

*"Vélodrome d'Hiver," a covered stadium for winter bike races, located near the Eiffel Tower. It doesn't exist anymore.

the children east. This meant filling out forms. That takes time. On the other hand, they couldn't let the trains leave France half-empty. They deported the mothers first."

"Without the children?"

"They kept them in Pithiviers, with a few mothers. And when Berlin said okay, they deported them. There were some in my train. These poor kids. . . . It was a pitiful sight."

"You were arrested after the roundup?"

"I had escaped to the Free Zone, but they caught me there."

"They arrest the Jews in the Free Zone?"

"They arrest them everywhere, except in America. Tell me, I want to know something. When we arrived in the Auschwitz railway station, the healthy men walked to the camp. Trucks carried away the children, the mothers, and the old people. I've heard that the Germans kill them with poison gas. Do you know anything about that?"

"What's for sure is that they vanish. There are single women in a separate camp, but nobody ever saw an old person or a mother with a child."

He says the Vél d'Ḥiv roundup was for foreign Jews only. This means my Rachel and my little Élie, who are both French, may have escaped. I have little hope when I think of Carole and Rose, the wife and daughter of my brother Jacques. Now that I'm stronger physically and mentally, I try to understand the logic of the camp. I talk to people, I ask questions everywhere I go. During my investigation, I meet a comrade who knew Jacques. I'm sure my brother is dead. He confirms it.

"After just twelve days, he was already a Muselman. He asked me what day it was. I told him. It was his daughter's birthday. He climbed onto the roof of an unfinished building and threw himself down headfirst."

If he had survived, I would have found a job for him in the clothes kommando. This wouldn't have helped much. He would have died of grief on discovering they were deporting women and children.

One of my comrades found two dresses belonging to his own wife in a bundle of clothes, then a little suit he cut himself for his son. He ran toward the fence so the watchtower guard would shoot him.

I work in the clothes kommando for some time. How long? In Auschwitz, we have neither clocks nor calendars. We're too tired to count the days.

Fall has come. . . . Or is it already winter? The summer heat is just a vague memory. It rains, it snows sometimes, it freezes at night. The prisoners who do not own good shoes catch frostbite that condemns them to death. The call at dawn, which lasts hours in temperatures around twenty, is a terrible torture.

One morning, we walk across the camp under a cutting sleet. If we didn't feel like tired robots, unable to raise our heads up or express any feeling, we would sigh with pleasure upon entering the Kleidenkammer. The room isn't heated, but its roof does protect us from the rain. Something is wrong, though. Our group isn't moving forward. I come out of my apathy and look up past the comrade in front of me. Hey, what does this mean? There are some guys already sitting at our table! Where are they from? Their skulls are shaved entirely. They are wearing heavy clothes that look like Russian uniforms. I see our kapo talking to their kapo. He turns toward us.

"These gals will replace you, shitbags!"

I take a better look at these beings with shaved heads. Women? Well, it is possible. They're awfully thin, like us. Those who have the runs don't exactly smell like roses. Their gray faces convey nothing. I have forgotten what women look like, but these creatures don't help much. The Germans always want to organize things better. They think that the women, with their natural skills, will be more efficient than us at unstitching the yellow stars and folding the shirts.

The marvelous German organization isn't that perfect. Otherwise, we wouldn't be standing here with nothing to do. They find a job for us: we carry the heavy pots full of coffee or soup. We know that we can't talk to the women if we want to stay alive. They do not look at us. They keep their mouths shut. Nevertheless, we hear a very low whisper: "We come from Bratislava, in Slovakia. . . ."

On the following days, I am back with a digging kommando again. The fine health I had gained in the clothing chamber runs out by and by. Laybich kicks me off my straw mattress. Back to nights with six comrades on a board. Back to hunger, thirst, fear.

I dream I'm sitting by my window in Praga, looking at the market. The peasant has spread some leeks carefully on the ground. I take a better look. The leeks are bodies, lined up in bunches of five.

CHAPTER 14

Little Rosenberg wants to show he's the best

It looks like our masters—SS and kapos—want to get rid of us to make room for the new guys. On Sunday, our "day off" without any kommando work, they keep us busy by stepping up sport sessions. I used to belong to a sport club. I practiced several sports for pleasure. In Auschwitz, "sport" is just another word for death. They force us to run naked in mud and snow, then they throw freezing water at us.

"At last you'll be clean, you shitbags!"

They club whoever doesn't run fast enough. We don't look like athletes on a track field, but rather like a flock of freshly shorn sheep running away from a pack of nasty dogs. In fact, the SS do threaten us with their German shepherds, Nazi brutes like their masters. They growl, bark, and show their fangs to keep us in line.

Our tormentors run us to exhaustion; then we stand for

hours while they count us. After such "sport," we can hardly sleep, either because we're coughing or because our neighbors are. On Monday morning, twice as many bodies as usual lie in front of the block. Before the end of the week, half of the block's inmates have become Muselmen and vanished. Some are killed by the kommando kapos because they are too weak to work, others are sent to block seven, where no one ever comes out alive.

Newcomers step off the train and replace our dead comrades. In the middle of a group arriving from France, I recognize little Rosenberg, who nearly broke my jaw when he came to the club as a kid four years ago. I stopped boxing soon afterward, but I heard he progressed so fast that Karl, our trainer, wanted to turn him into the champion of Paris or even of France. He is still very small—two inches shorter than me, I'd say.

"Hello, Rosenberg. Do you remember me?"

"Wisniak, my first opponent! How could I forget you? I heard they organize boxing matches, here. We could try to see if you can still dodge my punches."

"I'm not in such good shape. I'd be a lousy opponent. You just arrived. You're fit as a fiddle."

"You bet! I've never stopped training. I fought in the Free Zone. I had to change my name, because Jews are not allowed to box. Somebody denounced me. I don't even know who it was."

I notice that his number has six digits. I am an old-timer

and he is a just rookie, like that day in the club. I give him the usual advice: "Keep your shoes on at night," and so forth.

After four or five months, I am what we call an "old number." I belong to the "forty-eight-thousand" group, that is to say, the camp's aristocracy. There are not so many of us anymore. The comrade who told me about my brother's death belongs to the "forty-two-thousands," who arrived in June 1942. Some of the "twenty-eight-thousands" are still alive. Theirs was the first French train, which came from Compiègne in March 1942.*

Sometimes, we enjoy a quiet Sunday. If no new train is expected, they don't need to inflict sport sessions on us. We sit and try to get rid of some of the lice that swarm on our clothes. One lazy Sunday, a watchtower SS notices the squat shape and the big muscles of little Rosenberg.

"You, Jew! Yes, you, shorty! I'm sure you're a good fighter. Look at the guy sitting over there. Go ahead and fight, you two."

He points to a frail Muselman who's at least a head taller than Rosenberg. A terrible memory floats to the surface of my mind. They wanted me to hit a tall Muselman, too. . . .

---

*Thirty German criminals came from the Dachau and Sachsenhausen camps in May 1940 to build the fence. They were numbered one to thirty. Then Polish prisoners, mostly underground fighters, built the barracks and the watchtowers from August 1940 on.

That was long ago. I have seen several such fights since. Usually, the comrade who knows how to fight hits hard enough to knock the other guy down, but not to kill him, so everybody is satisfied.

The tall fellow turns toward the watchtower guard.

"You want him to kill me. Just because you're bored up there."

"Come on, how could he kill you? You're taller and stronger. You'll win, I'm sure."

Little Rosenberg wants to show that he's the best, that he could have become the champion of France. Who says Jews can't fight? He rushes and starts hitting the tall Muselman on the body and the head with both fists. He's just as fast as he was on the day he came to the club, but he has worked hard since then and has acquired sharp and deadly technical skills. All his punches reach their target.

While the prisoners watch this murder in bitter silence, the kapos and foremen shout and applaud: "Yay, shorty! Hit the stinking shitbag! Mash him up!"

After a few minutes, the tall Muselman falls down. We hear a loud rattle coming from his throat, so we know he isn't dead yet. The kapos send him to block seven.

Little Rosenberg raises his arms and laughs, as if he had knocked out the world champ. The kapos and foremen pat him on the back and compliment him, as if to say, "Good job! You passed your exam with flying colors. Welcome to our side!"

He is a poor twenty-year-old kid. He doesn't understand what's at stake. We feel sorry for him. Yeah, but now we can't trust him anymore. A few days later, he becomes an assistant deputy, Laybich's helper and a patent killer.

CHAPTER 15

I'll tell the kapo you studied electricity

If I stay in the digging kommando, I'll soon be too weak to escape death. Now that I've regained my will to live, I know how to proceed if I want to hold on until tomorrow, until next week. Health and willpower aren't enough. I have to look around, be on the alert, foresee what may happen. For instance, our masters hit us with their clubs from morning to night. I have to guess when blows are about to rain down, then try to run and dodge. I'm lucky. Boxing made me tough. I can take more punishment than my comrades. Even if I don't weaken as fast as they do, a day will come when I can't run anymore and I'll end up in block seven.

I forgot the most important thing: health, willpower, and alertness are useless if you don't have luck, lots of luck.

One morning, as I'm preparing to leave with my digging kommando, I hear a familiar voice.

"Hey, aren't you Wisniak?"

"Prager! I'm not sure I would have recognized you if you hadn't called me. You're wearing an armband! Foreman!"

"I am an electrical engineer. Remember?"

"I remember we used to swim together in the Marne. I thought you were a doctor."

"I do electricity work here."

"Listen, can I join your kommando?"

"Sneak into the line, quick. I'll tell the kapo you've studied electricity."

When we left France, we thought the Germans were taking us to a work camp. The sentence *Arbeit macht frei,* over the gate, seemed to confirm our assumption. We soon discovered it was just a big joke. They don't really want the Jews to be productive, otherwise why would they kill us as soon as we become good at a certain task? In most kommandos, actually, we have jobs that don't require much skill: moving stones, digging holes. The real workers are the kapos and foremen who produce corpses. While I decided to follow the electricians on a whim, I soon find out that this is my lucky break. In this kommando, the word *work* means exactly the same thing as in the real world that exists outside this hell. Prager is a real foreman, who doesn't kill anyone. The kapo, a German political prisoner, tries to keep his men alive because he needs their knowledge. What worries me at first is exactly how little I know about electricity. Sure, I installed it in our apartment in

Paris, but it's not the same thing as being a trained electrician. Actually, the trained electricians in the kommando need strong assistants to carry huge rolls of barbed wire and heavy tools. We are building a fence for a new camp where they'll keep Gypsy families.

Since our work helps the Germans, the kapo and Prager think we shouldn't be overzealous. We screw in china insulators, then unscrew them and screw them in again. The SS who oversees us from his watchtower doesn't notice anything. His only goal is to kill Jews.

Prager warns me.

"When he sees a new guy, he throws a cigarette beyond the barbed wire. 'For you, if you can pick it up!' he shouts. The comrade reaches across with his hand, bends down, slips his head between two wires. Then the SS puts a bullet into his skull. 'He attempted to escape!' he shouts. 'He attempted to escape!' He laughs at his clever trick. Do you see what's funny?"

"We're building a fence that's still unfinished, but if we step on the other side, we're attempting to escape, is that it?"

"Yes. Then I've seen him climb down from his tower to check whether he hit the center of his target."

The SS has had enough of this game. On my second day with the kommando, he tries a more ordinary one. He throws cigarettes on our side of the fence.

"These are for whoever will box!"

Instead of killing us himself, he hopes one of us will kill another. Why would we do such a stupid thing? For a few cigarettes? We rejoice that we've found a good kommando. We're not going to risk our lives for a handful of smokes.

Ha, but wait! Two guys I remember from Pithiviers (Czech Jews, I think) come forward, ready to fight to the death. Both of them box well, but one of them, who is taller, lands most of his punches. The smaller one howls with pain, stoops, and puts a knee to the ground. I watch from a distance while I work. In the meantime, the SS leaves us alone. After an hour or so, I see that the tall one has knocked out the small one. Is he dead—or only wounded and ready for block seven? He lies on the ground until the end of our workday. Two prisoners carry him away.

We've walked half a mile on our way back to the camp. Now that the watchtower guard can't see us anymore, the dead man stands up suddenly and laughs! We laugh, too, and applaud. Everybody thought the Czech Jews were fighting for real. These guys are real pros.

Our kapo is angry. He addresses the smaller man: "You, if you come back here tomorrow, the guard will recognize you. He'll know that we tricked him and he will kill us all."

"All right. I'll go with another kommando."

If he goes, we need someone to replace him. I talk about it to Brod.

"They don't kill us. They don't even hit us."

"I'm a tailor. My father was a tailor, and his father was a tailor. What do I know about electricity? As soon as I touch electric wires, sparks begin to fly everywhere. Oil lamps were good enough for me, I tell you."

"You'll only have to carry the wires. Come on!"

He joins our kommando the next morning.

About ten days later, they line us up for an inspection. An SS examines us, then picks out seven men. I have a feeling he's looking for people who're still in fairly good shape. He selects me, as well as Brod. He doesn't ask us whether we're trained electricians.

CHAPTER 16

We perceive shreds of screams, carried by the wind's uneven breath

We make up a small kommando, with no kapo to second our SS. He leads us to a camp annex, beyond the gate. Something is fishy. The SS doesn't shout, doesn't scold us for walking too slowly, doesn't call us shitbags. He explains, as if he were talking to friends, that we'll be able to eat, drink, and even smoke. And that after one week, our situation will improve yet again. We'll be able to wash and we'll receive new clothes. Next we expect he'll offer us women. Fishy and scary.

We reach our new workplace around noon. We discover two large rectangles, some sixty yards long by thirty yards wide, delimited by a furrow in the ground. Three poles with floodlights stand in the center and at the ends of the first rectangle. We're to dig them up and drive them back into the ground so as to light the other rectangle. One of us, a real electrician, ties special hooks on his hands and feet so he can climb to the top of the poles and remove the wiring.

We notice that the ground seems damp in places. We move toward the poles. Our feet sink into the mud. We wade in a red liquid. Blood!

The SS stays far away from us, more than forty yards. Maybe he doesn't want to soil his shiny black boots. Or he is scared. Seeing death face-to-face every day has toughened us, but we are scared, too. This is not an ordinary fear, but a kind of deep terror that paralyzes and silences us.

We move the poles and install the floodlights. This is easy work. It is over after two or three hours.

"See that shed?" the SS asks. "That's where you eat. Then you stay there. You don't look outside. Do you understand?"

We spend the rest of the day in the shed without doing or saying anything. I just exchange a few whispers with Brod.

"There are bodies."

"Hundreds. Did you see the size of the rectangles?"

"You could say thousands."

"The comrades who raised the poles . . . they're down there."

"We're next. They'll throw us in."

On the morning of the second day, we arrive much earlier. We find out that a kommando came during the night and excavated the second rectangle. It now resembles a three-foot-deep swimming pool bordered by mounds of earth. They lock us up in the shed right away, so we can't see whether there's anything in the swimming pool.

Yesterday, the SS said we shouldn't look outside the shed, but he doesn't say anything today. I guess it doesn't really matter, since we're going to die anyway.

All the prisoners know that the Germans murder old people and mothers with their children. We heard about gas as soon as we entered the camp, but we didn't know how the executioners actually proceeded. So here it is. From our shed window, we watch—as a feeling of dread tears our hearts—the grim spectacle of the Jews' extermination. We can see several small houses in the distance. We hadn't even noticed them on the first day, but the nearest one is quite visible. Two groups of naked Jews are walking toward this house. On one side, old men and boys. On the other side, women, girls, and babies. Twenty people altogether. I find it odd that they don't look worried. Four men dressed in white and two SS flank them. The Jews enter the small house. The SS close the door. An SS brings in a container that looks like a can of paint. We hear the muffled noise of a trapdoor closing. Then we perceive shreds of screams, carried by the wind's uneven breath. Brod, who has had a religious education, says he recognizes the prayer *Shema Israel:* "Hear, O Israel—the Eternal is our Lord, the Eternal is One."

The men in white live separately, in their own camp, but everybody has heard about them. They belong to the

Sonderkommando (the special kommando). They live in comfort, they eat as much as they want, they are gassed after three months. The SS promised us new clothes at the end of the week. They're white clothes.

While the Jews are dying in the small house, teams of men in white are laying rails between the house and the pit. Then they bring small flatcars, simple platforms on wheels, to the house's door. Breathing through a mask, they enter the house, load the bodies on the flatcars, and throw them into the pit. When it's over, they cover them with earth. In the meantime, huge fans, which roar like airplane engines, clear the gas. Thus, the next group of Jews will approach the house without noticing any foul smell.

The earth rectangle now looks just like yesterday's. We come out of the shed and move the poles and the floodlights to the next rectangle. Then we eat and spend the rest of the afternoon in silent meditation.

I remember a Greek Jew telling me about his kommando. They dug a huge pit every night. Nobody knew why. There were at least two hundred men. It took no time at all.

I guess this kommando digs at the beginning of the night. They start gassing the Jews before dawn. When we arrived, the pit was probably quite full already. We saw the gassing of the last group. The mothers, the kids. I would prefer them to shout and cry. The Sonderkommando men always remove the rails and flatcars before a new group is brought to the house. Thus, they can't guess what it is all about. They don't tell them they'll be poisoned with gas. I wonder what they do tell them. That the small house is a dining hall where they'll eat. Naked? No, it doesn't make sense. They had us undress when we arrived, so they could shave us. They disinfected us with a powder against lice. Yes, this is more likely: "You'll take a hot shower and then we'll disinfect you." So the people undress. Why do they need them to be naked? They want the clothes, that's why. When I worked in the Kleidenkammer, I thought that the clothes came from the suitcases left in the train. Now I understand that there were also clothes from the dead.

On the third day, we see that several old men refuse to cross the threshold. Maybe they've guessed why they're being pushed, naked, into a small house with an armored door. The men in white take them to the side. When the others are in and the door is closed, the SS kill them with a bullet to the head. The SS never kill anyone in front of the women and children, lest it cause a panic.

On the fourth or fifth day, our SS ceases to lock us inside the shed. We can walk around freely. He wants us to become familiar with our future job. One of us even enters the gas chamber to change a lightbulb. He talks to the men in white and confirms my hypothesis.

"They promise them a hot shower and a meal. They say, 'Hurry up and wash before the soup gets cold.' "

We gather near the small house when the men in white,

masks on, open the door and pull out the corpses. The naked bodies are so terribly entangled that they become one gigantic monster. We try not to think of the horrendous spasms that locked them in this manner. Wild, frightening grins distort the faces. The gelatinous globes of the eyes have jumped out of their sockets, the better to stare at us from the world of the dead. We hear sharp snaps and cracks: the men in white are breaking the bones to untangle the corpses before they carry them to the flatcars.

Most mothers grasp the neck of their child with clenched hands. They strangled their own kid to bring on a faster death. We mutter, "*Oy veh,*" a Yiddish cry that means, "Oh pain . . ."

We've seen thousands of corpses in Auschwitz. We're old numbers, all of us. We thought we had seen everything. Yet, on this day, we discover that there is no limit to human cruelty and pain. We know that we just crossed an invisible border. If we survive, we'll never be ordinary men again.

Many ancient myths tell of a character who sees terrible things or offends the gods, then becomes blind or turns into a statue. Will we lose our sight? Pierce our own eyes like Oedipus? We walk back to our shed without talking to each other. The next day, we do not go out, although the door stays open. We speak in whispers.

"Next week, we'll be dressed in white."

"From then on, three months."

"How do they put away the Sonderkommando? Do you think they gas them?"

"I'd prefer a gunshot."

"You can always run toward the fence if you want a bullet in the head."

"We can still escape. Or at least, we can try to find a way."

"Me, I'd rather stay. We're doomed anyway. In the Sonderkommando, I can drink and eat. I'll sleep in a bed, I'll wash, I won't get beaten anymore."

In our group of seven men, two say they prefer to stay. If we want to turn back into ordinary prisoners, we have to hurry. We still sleep in our usual block, but we know that any day now, they'll send us to the Sonderkommando's separate camp.*

---

*This chapter describes the situation in 1942, when there were five small gas chambers in Auschwitz. In the spring of 1943, it was decided that bodies would be burned rather than buried. Crematories were imported from Germany and grouped in a new building that included large underground gas chambers.

The new gas chambers bore signs saying "Bathroom." Sentences like *Rein macht fein* (Clean is healthy) were posted in the changing rooms. There were hooks for hanging the clothes. The enamel plate that showed the hook's number also said: "Remember your number!" The last thing the Jews did before dying was to remember the number of their hook.

In official documents, the Germans never mentioned gas chambers. They wrote "SB," for *Sonderbehandlung* (special treatment). In the camp, they were more cynical. They just said: "The shower." The prisoners had their own slang. The gas chamber was "the bakery," because of the ovens. The men in white were "bakers." An angry kapo would shout, "You'll all end up in the bakery! From here nobody gets out except through the chimney. . . ."

CHAPTER 17

Something must turn up before tomorrow

Now that I am in line for the Sonderkommando, Laybich treats me with the kind of respect that men condemned to death get in jail before their execution. He gives me back my straw mattress. I can even sleep all alone. I don't sleep well, though. I dream that my mother, Rachel, and my little Élie enter the small house. They're glad they'll be able to wash. Me, too, I want to enter the house and tell them to come out, but the door is locked already.

The last time, Laybich called me Wisniak. Now he wants to know my first name.

"Maurice."

"Maurice? Are you kidding? You mean Moshe!"

"Yes, Moshe."

"Listen, Moshe. When you're over there . . . If, some day, you never know . . . If they take me there to gas me . . . Find a heavy club and break my head with one blow. You're strong, I know you can do it."

He wants me to shorten his suffering. To act like the mothers who murder their own children. Do I love him like I love my own son? I hate him. He had already taken my number down to choke me in my sleep and line up my body with four others outside the block. I want the bastard to suffer. Or do I? I don't know. Revenge? Laybich is but a cog in the terrible machinery of the camp. He never decided to become a murderer. If the Germans hadn't started this war and created the abomination of Auschwitz, he would be a tailor or a salesman somewhere in Poland. These Nazis are the real murderers. Could I club someone to death, actually? A friend, to keep him from suffering? An enemy? A German? I've never killed anybody. I'm not as brave as the mothers. I can still hear the sound of the men in white breaking apart their stiffened fingers. . . .

Laybich acts like I already belong to the Sonderkommando. I don't and I won't. I want to survive and tell the world about Auschwitz. At least I'll try. This is what makes me different from Laybich. "We'll all die," he says, "but I'll die last." He kills the dying to postpone his own death. He kills out of despair, in a way. Me, I hope to get out. I refuse to become a murderer, since I intend to go back to Paris and live an honorable life.

Besides, these desperate killers don't always survive longer than we do. They fight to the death with knives in the barons' toilets, under the cold glare of the Russian war prisoners. It is said that Marek, our former block senior, was killed by an SS he had been peddling gold teeth to.

That an SS should kill his golden goose shows how crazy they are.

I need to be especially alert and wary. Today is our seventh day in the kommando. Something must turn up before tomorrow or I'm dead. I get up. I stand in the snow during the morning call. I drink the coffee. Nothing turns up. I go back to the kommando with my six comrades. We spend the morning in silence inside the shed. We hear muffled shots coming from the houses. Soon, dressed in white, we'll have to reassure the poor naked Jews so that they cross the deadly threshold without faltering.

We move the floodlights, then go back to the shed to eat. Just after lunch, our SS brings us back to the camp—as if he offered us an afternoon off to mark the end of our probation week.

I've been resting in my block for twenty minutes or so when the camp's loudspeakers bark an announcement: "Volunteers are required for a coal mine kommando. Anybody can apply, except for the seven electricians."

Without thinking at all, I run out of the block. Something has turned up!

As I'm approaching the kommandos' meeting point, I begin to think. What if our SS is there to check whether any of his electricians is trying to escape? Too bad. Even if my chances of success are low, it's better to try my luck than to do nothing and end up in white, which means certain death.

An SS doctor examines us, following the usual Auschwitz

procedure: we undress and show him our backsides, since Muselmen can be recognized instantly by their fleshless buttocks. He also asks us to jump over a two-foot-wide trench. What with my boxer's legs and a week of rest in the shed, I find it easy enough. Many comrades fail this test. In the end, the doctor keeps four hundred fit men.

I see a smiling face. Good old Brod! He seized his chance, too.

"Fancy meeting you here, Brod. You didn't fall in the ditch, with that fat belly of yours?"

"My legs were shaking. I wondered whether our SS was going to look for his electricians."

"We shouldn't get our hopes up. You never know what to expect here. Maybe they are recruiting men for the Sonderkommando. Nobody ever volunteers, so they invent coal mines as a ploy."

"So tomorrow, either we're dressed in white or we're coal black at the bottom of the mine! Or our SS catches us. In that case, he puts a bullet into our skulls. Then we're neither black nor white."

"He won't come. I know him. He didn't understand why the Sonderkommando scared us. He let us look at the gas chamber to help us conquer our fear. 'See, my friends, nothing frightening about it. The Jews walk calmly into the little house. They pray to their God and die; then you bury them. It is quite simple.' He's sure he cured us of our silly fear."

"He thinks we're eager to join the Sonderkommando?"

"Of course! Three months of comfortable living! He would prefer that to a day-by-day struggle for life with constant beatings. He can't imagine we'd choose the mine instead."

"Tomorrow, he'll be missing two electricians out of seven."

"He won't bat an eye. He'll think our block senior killed us for any old reason—or without any reason."

We walk out of the camp with the usual escort of kapos and SS. We're relieved to see that we go toward Auschwitz I rather than toward the gas chambers. We've made it!

I've spent five months or so in Birkenau, but I feel I've always lived there. My former world has been reduced to a vague memory that sometimes haunts my nights.

CHAPTER 18

I am not strong enough to vanquish the Polish blizzard

The distance between Auschwitz I and II is under two miles, but we need more than an hour to shuffle across. The icy December night is already falling when we reach Auschwitz I. We have to undress again to be shaved and deloused. Suddenly, after only three-quarters of our kommando have entered the delousing room, sirens begin to shriek: Air alert! Locking all blocks!

You can't always be lucky. I stay outside, naked in the cold air, with about a hundred comrades. We run every which way, looking for a block that might have kept its door open. Russian airplanes fly over the camp. Our chalky bodies glimmer like immense glowworms in the bright light of the Russian flares.

Driven by our survival instinct, we flock together to escape the cold. Every one of us tries to dive as deep as he can into the warm pulsating swarm. Being stronger than the others, I reach the center quickly. Just as quickly, without being able to react or realize what's happening, I am thrown back outside. Giant worms are entering the swarm in a constant flow, pushing and shoving, popping out, running around. I try shadowboxing to get warm, but I am not strong enough to vanquish the Polish blizzard. My blood is cooling. Soon I'll be stiff and blue, like the corpses I used to see on the bridge when I crossed the Vistula. I throw myself onto my comrades and rub my skin against theirs. I enter the swarm again, but I can't stop shivering.

After an infinite length of time (one hour? much more? much less?), the alert is over. The doors open. They shave our bodies and tear off our skin in the usual manner. On our first day in the camp, they sheared a strip of hair on our heads. Now they shave the rest. They immerse us into a vat of gasoline to kill the lice. The kapo advises us to close our eyes, but my eyes still burn when I come out. This is nothing compared to the maddening pain that gnaws the places where the shears tore my skin away, especially between the legs. Then we are entitled to a real shower. I mean, a real Auschwitz shower, with neither soap nor towel—a divine shower, the first for me since the clothing kommando. I say good-bye to the king-sized jacket I had received in that wonderful clothing kommando, which was turning slowly into rags. They give us shirts and uniforms that look like striped pajamas. I'm glad they allow me to keep my good winter boots.

In this part of the world, at the foot of the Carpathian Mountains, the winter temperature falls below zero. I wonder whether the pajamas can keep us warm. Right now, I'm burning and shivering, my head is spinning, I find it hard to breathe. I guess I caught a cold during the alert.

They let us sleep on the floor in the delousing block. I collapse and sink into a deep sleep. In the morning, I feel someone shaking me. I see a fuzzy face, as if through a thick fog.

"Is that you, Brod? Where are we? What happened?"

"Wake up, Wisniak. This is no time to be sick. Get up, quick. A doctor is going to inspect us again."

He helps me stand up. I've got to walk on my own two feet in front of the doctor. I'm lucky. This is not an SS doctor like yesterday, but a prisoner in a doctor's smock, supervised by a plain SS. He can see that I'm tottering and shivering.

"Do you want to go to the hospital or to the mine?"

I try to answer, "To the mine," but I hear that my voice has a mind of its own.

"I'm sick. Leave me alone."

I've lost control. My fever has taken over. The doctor seems angry.

"What kind of a joke is this? You're healthy enough to work."

The SS offers his own diagnosis:

"He's sick. Send him to the *KB.*"*

Suddenly, the doctor punches me in the chest. He doesn't hit very hard, but my legs are so wobbly that I fall to the ground. Instantly, I rebound like a spring. This is a camp rule: when you're hit, you get right up and stand at attention until the next one comes. If you stay down, you'll be kicked or clubbed to death. I don't stand up in obeyance of the law, but because I have acquired this reflex long ago, like all the prisoners who survived the fateful first three weeks.

The doctor turns toward the SS.

"See, he's very strong. He'll make a good miner."

My mind is all mixed up. I don't understand what's happening to me. I complain to Brod: "Did you see that swine? Hits a sick man! Calls himself a doctor. . . ."

"Don't you understand? He just saved your life! He saw your number. He knew you would get up."

We line up in rows of five and walk to Jawischowitz,† where there is a camp near the mine. The doctor was right: if I were really sick, I wouldn't be able to walk.

The SS guards who oversee us want to have some fun.

"You make too much dust when you drag your shoes, you shitbags. Take them off!"

We bruise and scrape our feet on the stones of the unpaved road. In spite of the pain, I keep on walking. The SS

**Krankenbau*, infirmary.

†Jawischowitz (pronounced Yavishovits) was the German name of the Polish town of Jaworzno (pronounced Yavozhno), located twelve miles from Auschwitz.

order us to walk faster. I walk faster. They order us to sing. I sing and I walk. They dole out blows to teach us how to sing in tune. I shake with fever, I endure the blows, I sing and I walk. I begin to weep like a child. Brod worries.

"Feeling worse, Wisniak? I've never seen you cry. Your feet hurt?"

"Until the age of six, I went barefoot. The soles of my feet aren't as calloused as they used to be, but I can take it. No, I'm crying out of joy, because we escaped the Sonderkommando."

CHAPTER 19

There's no patrol in front of the fence

After half a day's walk, we reach Jawischowitz. This camp is much smaller than Birkenau. There are other differences. They welcome us in a civilized manner by giving us "coffee." What's more, they serve it in regular bowls, not in chamber pots. As we're even more thirsty than usual, because of the road's dust, we rush toward the barrels. The Jawischowitz kapos slow us down with their clubs, but they don't kill anybody. We can enjoy a warm shower with soap. We sleep on straw mats. One man per mat. Paradise!

We don't go down to the mine right away, because they quarantine us. They want to check that none of us have a contagious disease. It would be bad for production if we spread diseases to the real Polish miners. Here, they do not produce corpses like in Auschwitz, but coal for the Reich.

During our quarantine, we dig trenches in the mud. It rains, it snows. We get a marvelous hot shower every evening, but afterward I have to put my wet clothes on again. They never seem to dry. It would be better if I was sandwiched between two comrades at night, like before. I am always cold. I don't eat enough to regain my strength. My fever returns, bringing along a nasty cough and my familiar companion, diarrhea. When I fall asleep, I see the gas chamber in my nightmares—the entangled corpses, the strangled children, the earth oozing blood. My will to live frays gently but steadily. I would like to die without suffering. I talk to Brod.

"Did you notice there is no patrol in front of the fence?"

"So what? Do you want to escape?"

"This is not like Auschwitz. You can throw yourself onto the wire without being bothered. You die at once."

"What are you talking about? We decided we would survive, don't you remember? We're going to tell the world what we've seen."

"They'll fix up this camp, put patrols and kommandos everywhere. Soon, it won't be possible anymore. We have to hurry."

"I wish you'd stop raving, Wisniak. Your fever is muddling your mind."

I get up in the middle of the night. I walk noiselessly across the sleeping block. Soon, I won't suffer anymore. Suddenly, a blow to the nape of my neck knocks me down. Someone drags me back to my bed. When I wake up for morning call, I remember vaguely that I wanted to walk out of the block, but I've forgotten why.

"Say, Brod, do you think you could knock a guy down with one blow?"

"Me? Certainly not."

"You boxed, didn't you?"

"That was a long time ago."

"Listen, I have a feeling that a comrade saved my life last night. If it was you, thanks."

Every morning, I am surprised—and relieved—not to see corpses lined up in bunches of five outside the block. In Jawischowitz, the sick are taken to a real infirmary. Nevertheless, out of the four hundred comrades in our kommando, one hundred become Muselmen after a few days, exhausted by hunger and the icy winter rain. They walk back to Auschwitz and the gas chamber.

At the end of the quarantine period, they check our health again. I've eaten charcoal to cure my diarrhea. I feel okay. Two doctors, an SS and a Polish prisoner, feel our muscles and look at our teeth, as if we were horses. They judge me fit for service. I hope to go down soon into the warm entrails of mother earth. In the meantime, we're still digging. The weather is getting colder every day. The earth is beginning to freeze. Shivering in our striped pajamas, we try to cut open the hardened ground with our picks and spades. The kapos hit us vigorously but not viciously. They just want to keep warm.

CHAPTER 20

An elevator that falls a thousand feet down

On the morning of our first day in the mine, the camp senior, a Polish criminal, delivers a short speech:

"You Jews, you've never worked in your life. I wonder how you'll manage in the mine. I'll pray to God and ask him to let you come up alive."

The mine is a half-hour walk from the camp. The SS guards who come with us stay above ground. Twenty of us huddle in an elevator that falls a thousand feet down in less than a minute. The plunge is so violent that I'm afraid my digestive tract will expel food at both ends.

Polish miners—that is, free people, who live outside the camp—welcome us at the bottom.

"So, you Jews, you ain't eatin' fat geese and honey cakes no more!"

Some of them kick us playfully when we walk in front of them, others just spit on the ground. We reach a kind of round chamber at the end of a long well-lit corridor. Dark tunnels branch off from the chamber in all directions. There is no more electric light, so we must turn on our headlamps.

Brod, a comrade named Gelber, and I make up a team. We will be helping two Polish miners—an old man and his younger assistant. Two black giants. The old man sighs when he sees us.

"Look at these Jews they give us! The three of them together weigh less than me. . . . Do you understand what I say, you midgets? Do you speak Polish?"

"Yes, we're Polish, all three of us."

"That's a good thing. Before you, I had some Dutch Jews who didn't understand a bloody word. Look, you have to shovel up these stones and throw them into the tipcart."

We're digging a gangway that leads to a coal vein. Specialists called blasters blow up the front of the gangway with dynamite. We remove debris, break rocks with pneumatic drills or pickaxes, shovel earth and stones. Other teams extract the valuable ore from the vein.

The young miner speaks some French, having worked in the mines in the north of France. He shovels up a hundred pounds of earth at a time and sneers when we can barely raise half that much. I do shovel up more than the old man. And besides, the young one stops often to rest. Then he watches the end of the tunnel for the foreman's light. Indeed, a faint glow pierces the darkness eventually. The old miner warns us:

"It's him!"

*"Le porion,"** the young man says in French.

We work faster. Just as I hoped, we're nice and warm in the mine. Our pajamas are as soaked with sweat today as they were with rain yesterday.

The foreman is here. He carries his lantern in one hand, an iron bar in the other one.

"How do they work?" he asks the old miner.

"Like Jews!"

The foreman expected this answer, I guess. He starts hitting me with his bar. I try to dodge, but his light blinds me. I twist and turn so he'll hit my shoulders and back rather than my head. After about ten minutes, he chooses Gelber as his second victim, but he is tired and doesn't hurt him too much. He turns toward Brod.

"Don't worry, you'll get it tomorrow. You'd better work, you stinking Jews. Especially you"—he points his finger at me—"because I can see you're stronger than the others."

When he's gone, I can't help weeping—for the second time since I've come to Auschwitz. I am covered with cuts and bruises. There is no part of my body that doesn't ache. With most of my flesh and muscles long gone, my bones are exposed. One of my shinbones hurts so much that I can barely stand up.

The young miner whistles to express his admiration.

---

*Foreman, in miners' slang.

"You, Jew, you're a strong one. You didn't even scream. The guys who were here before you bawled and fell down. . . ."

The old man keeps silent. It seems to me that he might be ashamed. I show my bruises to him.

"You really hate Jews! I don't think I worked so bad. Why did you want the foreman to beat me?"

"I didn't say you were a bad worker."

"*Work like Jews?* You might as well have told him we were lazy good-for-nothings."

"If you had started screaming like the guys who were here before you, he would have left you alone sooner. Look, now you're all bloody."

He isn't really mean. He lends me his tea bottle and his handkerchief so I can rinse my mouth. I also wipe my face, because the kapos hate the sight of blood.

No kapo notices anything. When we come out of the mine, we're covered with grime anyway. We feel human again after our warm evening shower! Even more amazing than the shower: they give us clean pajamas to sleep in. We use our mining pajamas as pillows.

Instead of eating in the block as in Auschwitz, we sit in a dining room. They give us a soup—which sometimes includes a floating turnip—and a spoonful of jam and margarine. Every now and then, we get a piece of sausage. This is supposed to make us strong enough to lift ten tons of earth and stones each day.

On our second morning underground, the foreman tells us our two miners don't need three helpers. He sends Brod to another team.

When we step out of the elevator, we see the Polish miners who kicked us and joked about fat geese yesterday. They stare at me as if I were some kind of ape. Nobody dares kick me. I don't know what I look like, since we have no mirrors, but I can guess that my face has swelled up and turned black and blue during the night.

The old miner didn't expect me to work. "When the foreman used to beat a Jew with his iron bar, the Jew would spend a few days in the infirmary. You didn't have to be back today already."

"I don't trust the infirmary. . . ."

"At least you can rest a little. If you see a glow at the end of the tunnel, start working."

Our two Poles rest more than a little. Digging a gangway is tough and uncertain work. You never know in advance what kind of rock you'll find. Then you spend lots of time waiting for the blaster, assembling venting tubes to draw up the gasses, setting up steel pillars to hold the ceiling, laying rails for hauling tipcarts called tubs. The gangway's progression is always quite slow, so the foreman can't expect us to move much faster. The miners who work in the coal vein have a very different job. They advance in a regular manner. If they tried to rest like us, the foreman would notice right away.

After a while, the old miner offers me a piece of bread and some bacon.

"No, thanks."

"Are you sure? Is it because of the bacon? You don't eat pork?"

"I don't believe in religion. I am not hungry. Give it to Gelber."

Of course, hunger never ceases to wrench my guts, but I have noticed that I often suffer from diarrhea after taking a beating. I'd rather be careful.

By and by, my pain subsides. A few days later, I accept the old miner's bread. We do not see the foreman for a whole week. Then he returns and asks the old miner: "So, how do these Jews work?"

"Just fine."

"See, these pigs have been idle all their life. The only way to cure their laziness is to give them a good thrashing!"

CHAPTER 21

I swallow six eggs with their shells

Although I supplement our pitiful meal with half of the miner's bread (Gelber eats the other half), I feel I'm weakening again. In Jawischowitz, they don't club prisoners to death, but they let them become Muselmen day after day. The end is the same.

The SS raise pigs in a corner of the camp. When they throw vegetable peels to them, the prisoners fight to catch a few.

The young miner suggests an exchange. "I bring you some food, you give me clothes."

I guess he worked out this type of barter with our predecessors. Clothes are easy to find in the camp, since suitcases full of them arrive every day in Auschwitz. I don't like the idea of a career in the black market, but I have no choice: if I don't find some food, I'll become a Muselman and go to the gas.

In the camp's slang, the verb *organisieren*, which is the same as our "organize," means "to find a way of getting." I organize a pair of socks by giving up a piece of sausage that comes with our soup. The prisoners usually go barefoot in their shoes, or wear rags called Russian socks. I put on the real socks to go down into the mine, then I come out barefoot. The young miner gives me half a loaf of bread and a dry sausage. I eat part of this treasure. I'll use the rest as currency.

On the following days, I bring down shirts and even blankets, which I wrap around my body. I get great quantities of food. I am very careful not to carry it up right away. Since they search us every three or four days, I wait until the day after a search. One evening, as I'm carrying a precious cargo, six eggs, I notice that we're slowing down as we approach the camp's gate. This means that the SS and kapos, who are no fools, have decided to search us two days in a row. Knowing this might happen, I always walk near the end of the line. If I throw the eggs on the ground, they'll punish us all. I don't hesitate more than half a second: I have to swallow them with their shells. I worry a little, not knowing whether this is possible. The first one slides down quite well, so I guess I can do it. The last egg drops into my stomach as we pass the gate.

The Polish miners are not supposed to feed us. When the kapos find pieces of bread in a comrade's pockets, they "give him twenty-five." This means twenty-five blows on the buttocks with their clubs. After such a beating, only a very strong man can avoid becoming a Muselman in a few days.

Some prisoners bring back cigarettes and vodka for the kapos and block seniors. They are exempt from the search, of course.

CHAPTER 22

The cooks get used to me

The six eggs leave a bitter aftertaste. Another time, I'll bring a piece of bread or sausage too big to swallow and they'll catch me. This smuggling is too dangerous. I'd better stop.

All the prisoners have to find food if they want to survive. Many comrades work in the mine at night and get another job when they come back in the morning. Some become servants for a kapo or block senior. They make their master's bed and wash his shirts for a few ounces of bread. Others help the shoemakers manufacture or repair boots for the SS. This task would suit me, since I know leather. I could even become a full-time shoemaker and stop going underground. Except I don't want to work for the SS. Too dangerous. The only way to avoid being shot by an angry—or playful—SS is never to go near any of them.

I remember my brother Albert, when he was still Anschel, looking for potatoes day and night. I try to put myself in his frame of mind. Where would he find food in this camp? Why, it's obvious: he would go hang around the kitchen and see what happens. As a Yiddish proverb says: "Whoever works in the beehive can hope to lick some honey."

I borrow a broom from a kapo's servant. I enter the dining hall without asking anybody's permission and begin to sweep. A Polish cook opens the window that separates the dining hall from the kitchen:

"You, Jew, what are you doing there?"

"I'm sweeping."

"Yeah? Okay. . . ."

He closes the window. I come back every evening after working in the mine. The cooks get used to me. They call me the sweeper. They give me some soup. They ask me whether I can bring up eggs and onions from the mine in exchange for a shirt. I promised myself never to carry eggs again, but I need this relationship with the cooks, so I bring back two eggs and two onions.

They give me work washing dishes. This is easy, because the prisoners lick their soup to the very last particle. I just have to rinse the bowls. There are so many of them that I ask Gelber and Brod to help me. Brod isn't too eager.

"Do you remember I was a cook in Pithiviers? This idea of yours, I tried it in Auschwitz. I managed to spend one day in the kitchen. I had hoped to be able to eat a little more than the others. All the cooks were Polish political prisoners, guys who had built the camp in 1940. They didn't want any Jews in the kitchen. I hid in a corner and left with only a few bruises. Another Jew was less lucky. They tripped him when he was carrying a barrel of soup. The heavy barrel fell on him and broke his arm. He was good and ready for block seven."

"Here, too, the cooks are Polish, but they treat me right, I tell you."

Brod and Gelber are so hungry they can't afford to be picky. They decide to come along. It turns out that Brod was right to distrust the Poles. They ask us to carry steel vats containing fifteen gallons of soup to the digging kommando. We have to load the vats upon a horse cart, then unload them at the work site. This is a very dangerous job. I go to the head cook and protest.

"The place is at least three miles away. Look at the lids. The rubber ring is cracked on this side and altogether missing here. The ride will shake the vats and spill the soup. They are full to the brim when we start out, so the kapos will surely notice that some soup is missing when we arrive and beat us."

"Hey, you Jews, do you want to work in the kitchen or don't you?"

I try to think up something.

"Could you give us some of the wax paper you wrap margarine with?"

"All right, but don't count on finding anything left to lick!"

I roll the margarine paper to make a new gasket, which I insert to replace the rubber ring of one of the lids. I lock the iron fastenings on both sides of the vat. We shake the vat to check that the soup doesn't leak anymore. It works!

With this invention, we earn the privilege of being tolerated in the kitchen—a place usually forbidden to Jews. We carry vats every day when we're back from the mine. The cooks give us soup, slices of dried sausage, plum jam. Nobody would call me fat, but at least I'm not starving. One big advantage is that I don't have to exchange clothes for food at the bottom of the mine, so I don't live in fear of sudden searches anymore.

Brod's mood lightens so much that he begins to crack jokes again. Having found a tiny morsel of meat in his soup, he asks me whether I know the story of the Jew who orders a steak in a restaurant. "He looks at his plate and begins to weep loudly. The innkeeper hurries to his table: 'Anything wrong, sir?' Still sobbing, the Jew says, 'When I think that for this tiny piece of meat, they had to kill a big cow!' "

Our two Polish miners are amazed when they see us working better every day. They think of Jews as merchants, unfit for manual labor. They don't understand that we're able to work more because we're better fed. In any case, they respect us and treat us as friends. We have become "their" Jews. Often, anti-Semitic Poles make an exception for some Jews they know personally.

The specter of death is no longer perched on my shoulder like a familiar bird. It still flies by now and then, just to show it hasn't gone away altogether. For example, the SS camp commander drinks too much vodka and wants to have fun. He wakes us up in the middle of the night for winter Olympics: running in the snow with a snarling dog at our heels and other sports.

"Faster, you shit buckets," he shouts. "I'll make you run till you're good and ready for the gas!"

After these nights, many comrades become Muselmen. Dutch or Hungarian Jews come from Auschwitz to replace them. The miners complain.

"We worked hard at training our Jews, and now you send us these clumsy fools who don't even speak Polish!"

The camp commander is afraid of the mine's director, who is his superior in the SS hierarchy, so he organizes these sport events less often.

Danger lurks inside the block, too, like in Auschwitz. The block senior and the deputy don't strangle twenty prisoners every night, like Laybich (prisoners coming from Auschwitz told me other thugs killed him, after breaking his arms and legs), but they know how to turn a man into a Muselman with a good beating. Although I'm an old number, a Jawischowitz veteran whom the kapos know and respect, I must remain as careful as on the first day—or maybe even more—if I want to keep the meager privileges I've acquired. A new deputy, Mandelbrot, wants to hit me with his club because I bring extra soup for the block from the kitchen.

"I didn't order any soup. Go throw it away outside!"

"I'll bring soup when I want to. You'd better mind your own business."

"Oh yeah? We'll see. . . ."

"Come closer and I'll knock you right down!"

I've taken so many blows that a few more won't make much difference. If I let him boss me around, I'll lose my authority. Mandelbrot is taller than me and has a club, but I'm confident I can handle him. I'm taking a huge risk, of course. I'm gambling that the block senior will take my side. He is a German who arrived from Auschwitz not long ago. He was starving. He became my assistant in the kitchen and I fed him. Belonging to the higher race, he didn't stay in his lowly position long.

The deputy hesitates. He wonders whether I'm bluffing or some higher power protects me. I seize the opportunity and send a direct hit to his jawbone that breaks two of his front teeth. Instead of retorting with his club, he goes to the block senior and whines. A few minutes later, I hear the German's loud voice.

"Where's the Hirenzine who hit you? Don't worry, he won't try that again!"

Here he is, whip in hand. Mandelbrot points at me. This is a critical moment. In the camp's hellish world, you gamble your life nearly every day. If I lose my bet, I die. . . .

The block senior laughs.

"So it's you, my cook? Give me a piece of sausage, ha ha!"

I hand him a piece of dry sausage. He cuts a slice for himself and one for me. Still laughing, he turns around and hits the deputy so hard that he knocks him down for the count.

CHAPTER 23

The Red Army is trouncing the Germans

No German goes down to the bottom of the mine. The Polish miners meet in the round chamber where the tunnels start from. They bring German newspapers, which I translate for them. I even draw maps on the ground. They call me Professor.

"They're stuck before Moscow, in front of Leningrad. But in the south, they're moving ahead. They want to capture the Caspian Sea's gas fields. The Russians hold on to the city of Stalingrad, on the Volga River. The Germans have been trying to capture it for months."

I'm playing a dangerous game. An informer could hide in the crowd and denounce me for turning the news into "communist propaganda," a crime punishable by death.

One day, toward the end of the 1942–43 winter, I read in the paper that "the cheating Bolsheviks, instead of accepting a fair fight, attacked us from behind in a cowardly manner. . . . They'll regret this low blow. . . . Our revenge will be grim. . . ." I shiver from head to foot.

"This means the Russians have surrounded them. This is the beginning of the end."

Soon, all the prisoners know that the Red Army is trouncing the Germans in Stalingrad. Will we be able to hold on until the end of the war? Will we see the Germans defeated? Every other week, an SS doctor checks our buttocks and sends fifty comrades to the gas. Whereas Polish Jews, protected by the miners, find food and withstand the sport sessions, most Dutch and Hungarian Jews become Muselmen after a month or two.

As if death were afraid we'd try to escape its clutches, it tries to catch us inside the mine. One night, while I'm working with a different team, I see a Polish miner tumble to the ground in front of me. I know what it is—a gas pocket! It may not be the same gas as in the gas chamber, but it sucks the life out of you just the same. I pull the miner out by his feet just in time. He seems to resent that a Jew saved his life.

Serious accidents happen every week. My old miner warns us:

"If you hear a kind of thunderous rumble, drop your tools and run to the nearest concrete shelter."

I think accidents happen even in well-kept mines. In ours, of course, nobody cares about the safety of Polish and

Jewish *Untermenschen.** Eventually, the thunder rumbles. Even before I've heard anything, the old miner rushes toward the shelter—which is not too far, luckily.

"Hurry up! Follow me!" he shouts.

The steel pillars that hold up the tunnel's roof fall down one after another behind us, as if some giant were knocking down bowling pins.

One gangway has collapsed. Our old miner leads the rescue team. Four men are missing: two Poles and two Jews, one of them my pal Brod. We knock on the venting tubes; they knock back. We dig as fast as we can. The earth that obstructs the gangway contains huge rocks, which we must break down with pickaxes. We install new steel pillars. The mine's technical director, a Pole, comes down and compliments the old miner for his speedy reaction. We reach the four men. The two Poles and one of the Jews are wounded. Brod, who was protected by a large rock, is unhurt. When we find him, he is fast asleep! We call his name. He wakes up and smiles.

"*Bonjour*, Maurice."

"Were you actually sleeping? I can't believe it."

"Why not? I shouted for a while, but nobody answered. I thought: 'Either my hour has come and I'm going to die, or it hasn't come and I'll live. Let's wait and see!' No other deep thought entered my mind, so I fell asleep."

---

*"Undermen." According to the Nazis, people who did not belong to the superior "Aryan" race were inferior beings, not quite human.

"The Eternal placed a rock above you to protect you," Gelber says. "This means that your hour hadn't come."

I find this way of reasoning perfectly stupid.

"Your Eternal lets millions die in Auschwitz and he decides to save our dear Brod? This doesn't make sense. The Eternal said: 'Thou shalt not kill,' but mothers can't help strangling their own children in the gas chamber. Brod was lucky, that's all. There's no more to say."

I guess we're jealous. What with night shifts in the mine, midnight sport sessions in the camp, wake-up calls at dawn, we don't sleep much. Brod managed to sleep at least two hours under his rock!

CHAPTER 24

Your son is the same age as my daughter

The earth rotates around the sun, undisturbed by the terrible pain human beings inflict on each other. The days become longer, the air warmer. We live as if outside time. Except for Sunday, our days are all alike. What is today's date? We left Pithiviers on July 17, 1942. Have we already spent one year in the camp?

The SS mine director loves making speeches. "You're just lazy Jews. . . . If you don't work harder, I'll send you back to Auschwitz, all of you. . . ." Toward the end of summer, instead of threatening us yet again, he brings us incredible news.

"I've pleaded on your behalf with the authorities. You'll be allowed to send a postcard to your family. You can even hope for an answer."

Have Rachel and Élie been caught? Are they still alive? Do they still live in our apartment? Maybe they're pretending they're not Jewish. In that case, a postcard coming from Auschwitz would put them in danger. I send the card to our landlord, a decent Frenchman whom I know and trust. If they've been taken, I'll still get an answer from him. I try out some sentences in my head: *"I'm in good health. I work in a coal mine. How are my wife and my son? I hope everybody is okay."* I must reassure her without alarming the censors who will read the card before it is sent. I have to write in German, because of the censors. I hope the landlord will find someone to translate it.

Brod, Gelber, and I discuss this postcard business while we bring the soup vats from the kitchen to the digging kommando.

"They know they've lost. The Russians will crush them. They have decided to stop murdering people. They want to look their best when the time comes for them to be judged."

"You're either a hopeless optimist or a real fool, Gelber. After what you've seen in Auschwitz, do you think they'll just stop on their own?"

"Wisniak is right. Some guys who just arrived from over there have told me that they're gassing entire trainloads of Jews. As defeat is drawing near, they're hurrying up. Time is short, so they're working twice as fast."

"Then why do they let us write postcards?"

"Maybe the director appreciates our work, after all. We

work so much that he is able to double his output. They still hope to beat the Russians. They need the coal for their war factories."

"Hey, Brod, do you think the director is a special kind of SS? He's just like the rest of them. If they really wanted to exploit the Jews' labor for their war effort, they wouldn't exterminate them in the first place. I'll tell you what I think. People in France are wondering about all these Jews who were deported to so-called work camps. Why have they never sent any news? This postcard business is just another deception."

"One thing for sure is that nobody's going to write about women and children being gassed as soon as they step off the train. No doubt our cards will help support German propaganda."

Toward the end of 1943, as we must endure the frozen breath of winter once more, I change blocks again. I've already spent close to one year in Jawischowitz. Whenever I change my shift in the mine, I have to work with a new Polish team and move to another block. Bill, my new block senior, is a bloodthirsty brute whom all the prisoners fear. His deputy has heard that I'm tough, so he wants to crush me. Soon after my arrival, he puts me on sentry duty after the night call. The block is always guarded at night against thieves. If an SS walks by, the sentry must stand at attention and shout the number of prisoners inside the block. The deputy chooses someone he wants to punish or test. It is hard to stay awake, but if you fall asleep you risk a beating and a one-way trip to the gas. To keep my tired body from sinking into sleep, I pace back and forth and count my steps. I see a shadow in the night, a dark outline coming toward our block, pitching and tacking like a listing sailboat. It's the ferocious Bill! I stand to attention instantly and I shout the number of prisoners. He sneers.

"All right, all right!"

His sinister grin sends shivers down my spine. I'll bet he is racking his vodka-soaked brain for some exciting new form of torture to try on me.

"Don't worry. . . . I can see you're scared. . . . Go and wake up my deputy."

"I'm here, Herr Blockältester!"

The deputy is ready to grovel in front of his master, like a dog who knows he made some bad mistake.

"Who posted Wisniak here? Is it you?"

"Yes, Herr Blockältester. . . ."

"On your knees, shitbag, and turn around!"

He gives him a vigorous kick in the ass.

"Herr Wisniak should not be on night duty! Do you understand?"

I don't like this. Such a sudden vodka-tinged affection seems highly suspect to me. When Bill wakes up in the morning with a dreadful headache, he'll see me differently. He'll punish me for presuming to be his friend. What's more, the deputy will make me pay for the kick he got because of me.

Bill turns toward me.

"Do you have a wife, Wisniak?"

"Yes, Herr Blockältester."

"Call me Bill. . . . Do you know that your son, Élie, is the same age as my daughter? Let's go and drink a toast to our kids!"

My heart knocks wildly in my chest. If he knows the age and the name of my son, it means that a letter arrived from France. Rachel and Élie are alive! I feel so elated that I am able to swallow a glass of a nauseating vodka that someone brought up from the mine.

The next day, as soon as I come back from the mine, I hurry to the camp's office. Rachel has sent not only a letter, but also a parcel. The commander's secretary, Karl Grimmer, is a German condemned for fraud. He is a very unusual German: he doesn't hit us or call us shitbags. He tells me I'm fortunate.

"The parcel is nearly empty, Herr Wisniak, because the Auschwitz postmen took their share, but at least it made it here. The postmen probably thought you were Polish, like them, because of your name. Your comrades are not so lucky."

It is true that I have a Polish name: *wisnia* means a cherry tree.

"If you want," he adds, "I can write in your file that

you're a *Mischling* (a half blood), born from a Catholic father and a Jewish mother. You never know. It could save your life someday."

This favor never helped me, as far as I know, but it stands as proof that there was at least one humane German.

CHAPTER 25

Herr Remmele is a boxing fan

The Polish miners talk about Christmas, then the New Year, so we know that the year 1944 is beginning. The German papers that we read in the round chamber become less precise. According to Karl Grimmer, the secretary, the Red Army is advancing slowly but steadily. They recaptured Kiev, the capital of the Ukraine, and are moving toward the Polish border. The English and the Americans have forced the Germans out of North Africa. They landed in Sicily and have already reached Naples.

The camp has a new commander. Even though I try not to go anywhere near the SS, I think I know them, after a year and a half. They don't really look like human beings, more like bad guys in a puppet show. Well, this new commander, Herr Remmele, amazes me. He gives new meaning to the word *vicious*. He lives with his wife and his daughter in a small house that looks over the camp. He comes out on the balcony, holding the hand of his six-year-old daughter, a blond angel dressed in a white frock. He shows the camp to her: here are the blocks, there is the infirmary, and that's the kitchen. . . .

"Look at these Jews! See how slow and clumsy they are. This is just plain laziness. I'll show you that they can move much faster. . . ."

He draws his gun from his holster and starts shooting at the prisoners. His drunken laughter is nearly as noisy as his gun. I run for cover, like everybody else. So I can't see if the blond child enjoys the game as much as her father does.

Herr Remmele is a boxing fan. He asks the SS to set up a fight. The SS ask the kapos. One of the kapos volunteers. He is a gigantic Pole, a former boxer whom we call Double-Nose because his nose is broken in a way that makes it look like he has two of them. Other kapos recommend me. My reputation as a boxer has followed me since the day I refused to kill a Muselman in Auschwitz. I also broke two teeth of a deputy a while back, I can't remember when exactly. I don't remember his name, either.

Thus, on a Sunday, while I'm talking with Brod, a kapo calls me out.

"You, Jew, do you know the kapo Double-Nose? He wants to fight against you. The camp's commander bought boxing gloves."

"Double-Nose is three times my size and my weight. In

boxing, there are weight categories. A flyweight can't fight a heavyweight."

"So you're scared? That doesn't surprise me. Boxing is a sport for men, not for Jews."

"Okay, I'll think about it. . . ."

"Yeah, why don't you think about it! For thinking, you're the best, but for fighting you're the worst cowards."

He shrugs and walks away. Brod smiles.

"I hope you'll accept, just to show these shitty Poles that Jews can fight."

"That won't be so easy. The man is a former boxer. In a real fight, if one of the boxers weighs five pounds more than the other, it is already a huge advantage. Here we're talking about a hundred pounds more. He's going to turn me into ground meat."

"He may have boxed, but I bet he was lousy. Otherwise, nobody would have broken his nose. I've seen you fight. You're quick, you can dodge his blows."

"Maybe, but if he lands just one, I'm dead."

"You've got to try. You risk your life every day, so it doesn't make much difference. Do you know the story of the Jew who is the caliph of Baghdad's buffoon?"

"No."

"The caliph condemns him to death because one of his jokes offended him. As he remembers with some fondness the many times the Jew made him laugh, he allows him to choose his way of dying. 'O great caliph,' the Jew says, 'your humble servant chooses to die of old age!' "

Brod talks to the comrades. They all say I should fight. Those who traffic with the miners promise to bring me the most precious foods: eggs and onions, even if it means risking their own lives. The soup and the pieces of sausage I receive in the kitchen barely keep starvation away. I need more food if I want to build strong muscles. Onions are even more useful than eggs, because they contain good vitamins. I've worked in the mine for eighteen months. The gangway I was digging with the old miner and his partner has reached the coal vein. Now I work at extracting the coal with Vitek, a Polish miner. The vein is two feet high. I crawl, I move on my hands and knees. I spend so much time kneeling that my knee joints are inflamed and quite sore. The prisoners suffer from all kinds of aches due to the lack of vitamins: abscesses, boils, carbuncles, pustules. If I do not eat some onions, I won't be able to move when I face Double-Nose.

I tell the kapos I accept Double-Nose's challenge.

"But you should promise not to retaliate and punish me if I win."

"Why would we punish you? It will be a fair fight. The stronger one will win."

They're so confident their guy is going to beat me that they're ready to promise anything.

Now I must train. The cooks let me jump rope with a

length of string. I shadowbox or I ask Brod to be my sparring partner. My reflexes are still there. Boxing is like swimming or bike riding—something you never forget. First of all, I have to improve my breathing so I can fight long enough to wear out my opponent. I wish I could run when we bring the soup to the digging kommando. This would be good training. Of course, I can't just decide to run in front of the SS who's watching us. I must wait for him to bring it up.

"Hey, you, the boxer. Aren't you training?"

He lets me hop on the path instead of walking. I am careful not to go too fast. If I catch up with his horse cart, he might not be able to resist the temptation of shooting me just for fun. "The Jew tried to escape. . . ."

The kapos choose a Sunday in February. It is too cold outside, so they set up the ring inside a block. Everybody says "ring," but it consists of four stools in the middle of the block. The whole camp is crammed inside the block, I think. Some prisoners are sitting on the beds; most are standing in the central aisle. The kapos sit around the ring. Fat and rosy, they tower over a flock of skeletons. It looks like they have absorbed all of our body fat. They shout, they joke, they laugh loudly.

I sit on one of the stools. Brod, who acts as my trainer, tries to encourage me.

"You're going to win for sure. All the comrades support you. Don't forget, you're fighting for them!"

Six or seven years have passed since the last time I stepped into a ring. I recognize a forgotten feeling: a knot that tied my entrails before a fight. Except this time, the knot ties every fiber of my body. I don't fight for some tin medal, but for my very life. What's more, I defend the honor of my comrades and of my people.

Double-Nose sits down in the opposite corner. He wears black satin boxing shorts and sneakers. I've removed my striped jacket. With my pajama pants and my winter boots, my small size, and my meager body, I feel utterly ridiculous. I look like Charlie Chaplin trying his hand at boxing.

I hear a kind of hubbub behind me. The crowd parts suddenly. The camp's commander and his assistants have come to see the show. At least he hasn't brought his daughter.

We're just waiting for the referee. Here he comes. He enters the ring, turns toward me, and grins in an exaggerated fashion so as to show me his teeth. Two are missing from his lower jaw. He is the deputy I knocked down! I remember his name now: Mandelbrot. He calls us into the ring and introduces us.

"On my left, Herr Korzeniowicz. On my right, Herr Wisniak. The fight will last three rounds of three minutes each."

The kapos and the SS laugh when Mandelbrot introduces me. The comrades are not laughing.

Mandelbrot bangs on a tin cup with a spoon to start the fight. Without waiting, Double-Nose rushes at me and tries to hit me with both hands. My fear vanishes instantly. Brod was right: this guy really can't box. He seems to throw punches at random. His steps are as heavy as a bear's. He shouts like a lumberman wielding an ax. I may not jump around as lightly as I did ten years ago, but I move faster than he does. I dodge his punches by twisting my body, by moving my head back, by bending down to slide under his guard, by stepping aside. My relieved supporters begin to laugh at him. I'm not worried anymore. Double-Nose becomes angry. He puts all his energy into a punch that misses. He loses his balance and falls forward. Even the kapos and SS can't help laughing. He stands up slowly, muttering and swearing, then puts up his guard again.

The first round is over. I look at Double-Nose on his stool. His breathing is labored. He looks like someone who is learning to swim and just swallowed some water.

"He's done for," Brod says. "He won't last until the end of the second round. But you, Wisniak, you should be careful. Keep your distance."

The referee bangs on his tin cup. I stand up. Double-Nose jumps at me like a tiger. His strength is back. He isn't breathing like a drowning man anymore. He hits lower, so I can't slide under his guard. His trainer gave him some advice, obviously. He's still so slow that I can run circles around him. My comrades' laughs make me so confident that I laugh, too. I think that I'm keeping my distance, but I forget that my opponent has longer arms than me. He succeeds in hitting me on my side, near the liver. I wasn't tightening my abdominal muscles enough. Or maybe he caught me with a low hook. A sharp pain cuts across my stomach. I feel I'm falling to the ground. I think about death, my familiar companion in Auschwitz. A stranger saved my life when I had lost my will to live. Brod kept me from running to the fence. I've seen thousands of corpses. If I don't get up, I'll become one of them. Get up, Maurice! Gather the shards of your will and stand up. You've got to. While I'm talking myself into controlling the pain, I discover that I'm actually standing up. My body responded to the Auschwitz reflex and stood up without consulting me. My legs wobble; I start to swing as if I had drunk too much. Instead of finishing me off with a flip of his finger, Double-Nose gapes at me without moving. He can't believe I survived such a blow. I don't need more than a few seconds to collect my thoughts and step back.

After ages, Mandelbrot bangs the end of the second round. I wonder how he counts the three minutes without a watch. I think he waited for at least six minutes, leaving Double-Nose plenty of time to crush me.

Brod gives my poor body a vigorous rub.

"He got you good. Does it hurt?"

"I'm okay. . . ."

"Breathe deep. The massage will pep you up. You can make it. I'm sure you were hit even harder when you boxed in Paris."

"Don't worry. I'll be more careful."

"Double-Nose is exhausted. Now's the time to attack. Give him your all. This is the last round of your life, Wisniak! Look at the kapos and the SS. They're as white as bedsheets, because they know they've lost. We're counting on you. . . ."

At the bang of the spoon, Double-Nose rushes once more, but he doesn't know where he's going. He raises his arms in front of himself like a blind man. He wants to catch me so that I can't escape him again. He's pathetic. His arms drop down. He's so weak he can't keep his guard up anymore. I begin to throw hard punches to his body, then to his face. I put more power into them. Jabs, hooks, uppercuts. What's obvious is that he's used to being hit. He resists, he stays up, he tries to hold on to me to avoid falling. I push him away. He slides down gently and sits on the ground.

The referee doesn't know whether I'm allowed to knock out a kapo. He counts to ten as slowly as if he didn't remember the numbers. He could count all the way to a hundred—Double-Nose won't stand up.

The comrades shriek wildly. Whereas the kapos keep silent, wondering how to react, the SS applaud me and shout: "Bravo!" The kapos, following their masters' example, applaud shyly. I'm amazed when Double-Nose, standing up eventually, pulls me into his arms and pats my back in a friendly manner.

CHAPTER 26

We pass the camp gate in the middle of the afternoon

During the year 1944, I work in the coal vein with Vitek. This man is different from the other Poles—he doesn't hate Jews. The mine's director wants us to extract twenty tons of coal every day. To reach this monstrous goal, we must become a strong team and avoid quarreling. If we don't learn to coordinate our moves, the conveyor belt that takes the coal away can snatch us and carry us to disaster. Vitek and I become real friends.

"I've worked with several prisoners," he says. "They each held on a month or two before vanishing. I believe they're all dead. You've been here six months and you're still alive. How do you explain it?"

"At night, after the mine, I work in the kitchen, where I can eat a little more than the other guys."

"I can't believe it! You work here on your knees for eight hours, then you've got enough strength left to begin another job!"

"All the prisoners must find something if they want to survive. In the camp, rest doesn't exist. The Germans think there are too many Jews. Every other week, they select the exhausted ones and send them to the gas chamber in Auschwitz."

"Yes, I've heard about that. Other prisoners told me the same thing."

In June, the camp secretary informs us that the Americans have landed in France, on the Normandy coast. On the other side of Europe, the Russians are reaching the Polish border. For the first time since I arrived in the camp two years ago, a feeling that resembles a glimmer of hope lights my heart. The Germans will be vanquished soon, no doubt. If only we could manage to survive until their defeat!

They send the most ferocious SS to the Eastern Front, which gets closer every day. To the German prisoners who wear the green triangle of common criminals—that is, the main kapos and block seniors—they offer freedom if they agree to enroll in the army. The remaining barons, Poles or Jews, treat us with a courtesy that increases every day. They look like wolves wearing a lambskin. A kapo who is probably preparing to escape forces me to give him my winter boots, which I had been able to keep all along. Now I wear canvas shoes with wooden soles.

Toward the end of the year, we stop going into the mine. The Russians have taken Warsaw. When the wind blows from the east, we hear a vague rumbling—the song of their cannons. What will happen to us? The pessimists think the Germans will kill everybody before leaving. The optimists expect the Red Army to free us before the end of the week.

In January 1945, we learn that we'll neither be gassed nor liberated by the Russians, but "evacuated." One morning, they give us each a blanket and a piece of bread. Every prisoner is also entitled to a dried sausage. The barons keep all the sausages, as if to stay in character until the bitter end. Standing in rows of five, we wait for hours in the cold. Brod and Gelber are with me.

Two SS go to the infirmary. "We advise you to come with the others," they tell the patients. (I know this because Finkelstein, a comrade from my block who broke his leg when the conveyor belt caught him, told me about it after the war.)

Ever since we've been hearing the rumble of the Russian cannons, the SS and the barons seem to hesitate before committing their usual crimes. Still, Finkelstein and our other bedridden comrades distrust these murderers. The two SS seem to imply that staying would be a bad idea. "Is it a good old death threat?" Finkelstein wonders. He tries to stand up but can't. He doesn't have a choice: he must stay on his straw mat. "I've been very lucky so far," he thinks. "If the SS hadn't grown soft suddenly, they would have cured my broken leg in the gas chamber. . . ." (He stayed ten days in the infirmary; then the Germans vanished and the

Russians freed him. In the meantime, all the evacuated invalids died.)

We pass the camp gate in the middle of the afternoon. Daylight is already receding. We walk on a narrow road, toward an unknown destination. The barons have loaded their possessions and food supplies on long sleighs. As horses are scarce, ten prisoners pull each sleigh.

The narrow road merges into a larger one. A pitiful gray procession crawls along it. Thousands of men and women try to resist the frozen wind. I recognize the tired shuffle of the Auschwitz prisoners. We stop and wait several hours. I guess we're supposed to walk behind them. They seem to slow down. The barons and the healthier prisoners marched in front. What we see now, under the bleak winter twilight, is the desperate parade of the sick and Muselmen.

One hour or so after the last Auschwitz Muselman creeps away, they order us to move. We hear gunshots far ahead in front of us. Brod and Gelber rejoice.

"The Polish underground fighters are attacking the SS. We'll soon be free."

"Or it might be the advance troops of the Red Army!"

These two poor guys are dreaming.

"Do you really think that the underground fighters or the Russian soldiers would shoot at SS in the dark? This would end up killing the prisoners. Besides, the SS would shoot back and we would hear machine guns."

"So what do you make of it?"

"Do you think the SS . . . ?"

"Of course. Listen to the shots: one at a time. They shoot the sick and the Muselmen whenever they stop walking."

"We should see bodies on the road."

"They push them to the sides. If there was any light, we would see them."

After a while, we also hear shots behind us. Brod wants to know for sure, so he begins to slow down. One hour later, he catches up with us.

"As soon as a guy lags behind, they put a bullet into his head. Remmele, the commander, and other SS take care of it. They ride motorbikes with sidecars. They find the stragglers with their headlights."

Russian war prisoners attack the Jews to steal their bread. Me, I ate my piece right away to be safe. The Jews resist; a fight begins in the dark. One of the motorbikes comes by. The SS shoot in the direction of the fight: three Russians killed and seven Jews.

Old German reservists, some of them more than sixty years old, guard our convoy—one soldier every thirty feet, under the supervision of the SS on their bikes. They walk, like us. At first, they carry heavy backpacks. Then they find it more convenient to use prisoners as mules. So here I am, bent under a huge bag, sinking to my knees into the snow. The white powder sticks under my wooden soles. I slip, I stumble, I'm finding it harder and harder to walk. I feel my legs getting weaker. If I don't discover a way out of this mess, I'll drift to the back of the line and the SS will kill me. I step on something. . . . A backpack! Of course: I'll just throw my bag away. I've wrapped my head and shoulders in my blanket against the cold, so I can hope the old reservist who gave me the bag doesn't recognize me. He saw me briefly under the glare of his flashlight. All the prisoners look alike, with their striped pajamas and shaven heads. I must take this risk to survive. I explain my plan to Brod.

"Just walk behind me and empty the bag. . . . When it's flat, we'll remove it more easily and just let it slide to the ground."

"All right."

I hear a muffled but joyful scream:

"Look at this, Wisniak!"

He shows me two whole sausages, two hard-boiled eggs, and a loaf of bread! We share this bounty with Gelber and several other comrades. After less than a minute, not a single bread crumb is left to incriminate us.

They order us to sit in a circle in the middle of a field. So far, it has been very dark because we were walking in a forest of firs or pines. Now our tormentors can see us clearly, as the snow reflects the moonlight. The motorized SS start shouting and shooting at us.

"Is this what you call a circle, you pigs?"

"Hurry up!"

"See, you can move faster!"

I think our number has been halved since we left the camp. I am so tired that I fall asleep instantly, sitting on my folded blanket.

Gunfire wakes us up at dawn.

"Up, up, you shitheads! By fives!" the SS holler.

Many comrades, frozen stiff, fail to stand up. The SS and the barons slept in a farmhouse at the edge of the field. Forty or fifty prisoners hid in the farm's attic to escape from the cold. The SS shoot into the straw to dislodge them. A dozen or so get out alive.

The old reservists tell the SS that their bags full of food have vanished. The SS decide to search us before setting off. When they find a lump of sugar or a piece of bread in a comrade's pocket, they tell him to stand to the side with the prisoners who are too tired to walk.

"Trucks will come and pick you up," they promise.

We never see any of them again, so we think the SS killed them. One third of the survivors disappear this way. We march all day. We pass through several villages. We see Poles watching us, hidden behind half-closed shutters. Brod is still looking for the underground fighters.

"I don't understand why they don't attack now. It is daytime."

"They're glad the SS are taking us away. You remember Krzisztof, the kitchen kapo? One day, we had a talk about escaping from the camp. He told me the Jews were better off staying inside: 'If you go out, the Polish underground fighters will bump you off. They want to create a new Poland without any Jews.' "

As the night is falling again, we reach the city of Wodzislaw. We have walked twenty-five miles or so. A train of platform cars is waiting for us in the station. New SS guards, needing to warm up, welcome us with whips and clubs. I stay on my feet and climb up on a platform. Many comrades fall repeatedly and receive harsh blows. A familiar voice calls me. I recognize Gelber, although his face is puffed and bloody.

"They really beat you up, Wisniak!"

"Me? No. I don't think they did. . . ."

"You're all black."

"Oh. Yesterday I threw away a reservist's bag. I didn't want him to recognize me, so I rubbed mud all over my face."

The train runs and puffs through the night. A thick layer of snow covers us and protects us from the cold. At dawn, we halt in a station called Buchenwald. The SS wake us up with the butts of their rifles. Some comrades refuse to wake up. The snow wasn't thick enough for them: they're as hard as stone statues.

CHAPTER 27

When I say hi to these Germans, they don't answer

The camp of Buchenwald is located in Germany, four hundred miles west of Auschwitz. A surprise awaits our barons: they lose their privileges. While we're standing on line for our first soup, one of them tries to overtake us. A Buchenwald deputy stops him:

"What do you want?"

"I am German."

"So what?"

"I am German and they're Jews."

"Here, you're nothing."

The deputy gives him a couple of sharp slaps, then sends him to the end of the line. Here, everybody receives the same allotment of soup. Later on, a Buchenwald prisoner tells us what happened in this camp.

"There was a kind of civil war. Political prisoners, mostly communists from Germany and other countries, have supplanted the German criminals who held the power positions at first. The SS went along with the change because the politicals could organize the camp better than the criminals. The Germans want their slaves to be as productive as possible."

What a pity: we can't stay in this paradise. It seems we're needed in another camp. After a very short night, they order us lined up by fives. I try to hide under a bed at the end of the block, but they find me and I hit the road with my comrades. The Buchenwald prisoners told us that the American army entered Germany. The great Reich that was supposed to last one thousand years is seeing its last days. This doesn't stop the SS from shooting the laggards as they did on the road from Auschwitz. We walk thirty miles toward the south, which means hundreds of comrades die on the road.

We enter the camp of Ohrdruf at dinnertime. They lead us to an annex of the camp called Krähwinkel. We miss Buchenwald. Here, the barons are criminals. They serve a watery soup in dirty cans that remind us of the Auschwitz chamber pots.

They tell us we'll be digging galleries in the mountain with German workers. I hope we'll be able to work together as well as we did with the Polish miners.

I sleep in a concrete blockhouse, for some reason the only Jew in the middle of one hundred Russian war prisoners. They push me to a corner, far from the single window, so that I have a hard time breathing.

"You shouldn't complain," they say. "Your friends are sleeping outside in the mud."

I only spend a few hours in this concrete box anyway. We leave before dawn; we travel by train for several hours to reach our work site. They carry us in tipcarts similar to the mine's "tubs." Triangular buckets are not a comfortable way to travel, especially when you put fifteen men in them. We're squeezed so tight that each of us can stand on only one foot. Some comrades scream with pain when cramps contract the ghostly muscles that stick to their legs.

We dig an underground factory. The Nazis want to make new flying bombs there. I carry a giant drill on my shoulder, with a six-foot bit, which two German workers push into the rock. After a few seconds, I am covered with dust. Stone chips hit my face all the time. The German workers wear helmets and goggles. As for me, standing in front of them like a human shield, I have no protection. These workers insult me when I stop to wipe off the dust. When they pause for lunch, they eat and drink as if I didn't exist. I work for eight hours without ingesting anything but the dust that parches my throat. Although the Polish miners were anti-Semitic, they reacted like human beings. As we worked together, they decided eventually that I was a man like them. They gave me water and even food. In the morning, when I say hi to these Germans, they don't answer. They treat me like a dog. Or rather, like what I am: a slave. They're no different from the SS.

At the end of the second week, a stone chip flies into my right eye. They forbid me to stop.

"Go on working, shitbag. Close your eye!"

So what? Do you think you'll win the war with your flying bombs? I'm lucky that the workday is soon over. As I'm leaving, one of the two workers tells me to go to the infirmary and show someone my eye. It is the first time they say something to me that is not an insult. It means they need me. I guess the Jews who preceded me were too weak to carry the machine for eight hours. If they lose me, they'll have to carry it themselves.

I know the doctor: Gamkhi, a Greek Jew who comes from Jawischowitz like me.

"The cornea is barely nicked, but you must be careful. If an infection sets in, you may lose your eye. All I can do is dress the wound."

He dresses the wound in the camp's usual manner, with a small square of toilet paper.

"I wish I could stay here for a few days. You could watch my eye and I would rest. I have to carry a very heavy machine, but I am not eating enough. I'm getting weaker. If only I could sleep a little. . . ."

"Look, this block is full of badly hurt men, many dying. If an SS doctor finds out I am keeping you here so you can rest, we'll both be in trouble. They watch me because I am a newcomer. Maybe I can take you in next week."

"What kills all these guys?"

"Exhaustion. They've reached the end of the line, you know. . . ."

I go back to work. Every evening, I show my eye to Gamkhi. He changes my dressing, which turns black because of the rock powder.

I run into Brod.

"Where have you been, Wisniak? I haven't seen you for a long time."

"I live in the blockhouse with the Russians. Also, I spend lots of time in the infirmary. I've hurt my eye."

"Stone chip? The war is nearly over, but these bastards will torture us to the bitter end."

"If we survive to the bitter end."

"You're right. Too many comrades weaken and die in this camp. Listen: I've thought of a plan. I've told Gelber and four others about it. We'll need another seven or eight. We climb together into a tipcart and remove the hooks that hold the bucket straight. You remove the front hook, I remove the back one."

"The bucket will flip and we'll fall!"

"That's my plan. If the accident happens right when we leave the station, before we reach our regular speed, we'll be hurt just enough to go to the infirmary."

"Pretty clever. . . ."

Brod's plan succeeds perfectly. We suffer from light bruises, but our boils and abscesses burst so that we are covered with blood. The SS run toward us with their whips, but they can't stand the sight of blood.

"Go to the infirmary, you stinking Jews," they shout. "Quick!"

Gamkhi, whom I've informed about our plan, shows us a wooden board in a corner of the block. We clean our wounds. This means that we wash for the first time since we left Jawischowitz. Then we lie down on the wooden board, pressed close together. I sleep for forty-eight hours straight—waking only for soup. After four days, my comrades go back to work. Gamkhi keeps me because of my eye.

"The wound doesn't really justify it. I'll give you a job. I need an orderly."

Close to three years after my arrival in Auschwitz, while I expect that I'll soon leave the hell of the camps forever, I'm back to the same task I was given on my first day: I carry corpses. A man is sitting on his straw mat, on the upper berth. Suddenly, without a word, he tumbles to the ground. He's dead. I go pick him up.

"Our block senior sends us to the infirmary when we're kaput," his neighbor says. "Ten of us came here this morning to see the doctor. Three are dead already and he hasn't even examined us."

I carry thirty bodies every day. The Russian war prisoners have stolen all the blankets. They tear them into pieces to make shoes. The sick men use the straw mats as sleeping bags against the cold. When they die, I must pull them out of a straw cocoon soiled with their piss and shit. Often, I need to break their bony fingers, which hold the cloth with a desperate grip. It is not true that I'll soon leave the hell of the camps forever. I'll never leave. I'll be a Häftling, a camp prisoner, for the rest of my life. I've become numb. Otherwise, my job in the infirmary would make me crazy.

One week after us, other comrades hoping to rest in the infirmary provoke a tipcar accident. The SS were willing to believe it once, but not twice. They send their dogs to check whether the accident victims are really unable to stand up. The poor guys come to the infirmary on stretchers. Torn flaps of skin and flesh hang from their thighs like wallpaper coming loose. Four of them die within the first hour.

I turn to Gamkhi.

"I thought I had seen everything!"

"Yeah. I don't know how many times I've had the same thought. . . ."

One of the wounded describes the dogs' rush.

"They attacked as if they wanted to eat us alive. The SS found it hilarious. I could see both the fangs of the dogs and the teeth of the SS. They were laughing like kids."

Gamkhi dresses the wounds with toilet paper.

It seems that the SS, feeling death closing in on them,

want to bring along as many people as possible. Two or three bodies hang from every tree in the camp. Hanging is the usual punishment for trying to escape. Russian war prisoners, hearing that the Red Army has entered Germany, can't resist the temptation.

CHAPTER 28

What do they want? Tell me, Wisniak. . . .

Around April 4 or 5, some two months after we arrived in Ohrdruf-Krähwinkel, they evacuate us again.*

We return to Buchenwald. Thirty miles on foot, without eating or drinking. This is the very heart of Germany. We're very close to the city of Weimar, where the great poets Goethe and Schiller lived. When we pass through a village, the people insult us and spit at us. I remember a village we crossed soon after leaving Jawischowitz. The Poles watched us in silence. Some of them looked at us with a kind of compassion or pity.

We have been fed so little that we find it hard to walk. What's more, the SS seem to be in some kind of a hurry. We hear more gunshots coming from the rear than before.

---

*Ohrdruf was the first concentration camp liberated by the American army—on April 6, 1945.

My knees and my hip joints hurt terribly. I must summon my willpower to keep from screaming with pain and lying down on the road. I mutter under my breath: "You've held on for so long, Moshe. It would be silly to give up now. Come on, one more step. And another one. . . ."

As soon as we pass Buchenwald's gate, I collapse on the ground. I see my comrades fight for a barrel of soup. It falls over. They lap up the soup mixed with mud, like animals.

Comrades carry me to a block and sit me down in a corner. I fall asleep right then and there. The next day, I hear rumors that the SS want to evacuate the camp. I can't walk. This time, I'll die.

Two days later, I can bend my knees. I can stand up. The Buchenwald men are dreamers.

"The Americans will free us any day now," they say. "We've decided to wait for them. We'll refuse to be evacuated."

The Jawischowitz comrades and I are too weak to oppose the SS. On the afternoon of April 10, they order evacuation.*

"Line up by five, you shitbags!"

We walk for hours. When my legs won't carry me anymore, I'll stop. . . . To my relief, we come to a railway station, where a train is waiting for us. Brod is there, as weak as me but still alive. We climb up on a flatcar.

---

*Having refused to obey the SS and be evacuated, the Buchenwald prisoners liberated the camp themselves on the next day, April 11, a few hours before the American army arrived.

"What do they want? Tell me, Wisniak. . . . The Americans and the Russians have captured most of Germany already. Do they want us to work still more?"

"They don't give a damn about the Americans and the Russians. They've always believed their real enemies were the Jews. Look at the SS on that passenger car's roof. . . . They're aiming their machine guns at us. Ready to shoot at the dying and the dead."

. . .

After a few hours, fifteen comrades or so are dead already. Others call out to the SS.

"Hey, we have some dead."

"Good. You're here to die."

"Where are we going?"

"Shut up, you stinking Jews, otherwise we'll shoot."

The next day, old reservists replace the SS. They give us bread—a quarter pound each. They only know the number of men at the beginning of the journey, so we also eat the bread of the dead. This is not enough, though, since we get nothing to eat or drink for days afterward. The train moves slowly, stopping often. Like my comrades, I spend my waking hours crushing the lice who've been feasting on my flesh since we arrived in Krähwinkel.

We halt in a station. I notice something strange: the Germans don't insult us anymore. They don't laugh at us. We read fear on their faces. Children wearing uniforms are waiting on the platforms. We ask our old reservists for water. We're amazed—they obey us!

The train starts again. Fifteen minutes later, low-flying airplanes come and shoot at it. Our old German guards jump down and hide under the cars. The Russian war prisoners—and some forty Jews strong enough to step off the train—scatter on both sides of the track. As soon as the planes vanish, the old soldiers emerge.

The lone SS commander is furious.

"You're not real Germans, you're cowards! Shitbags! You've let the prisoners go. Run and catch them at once. Pull a stunt like this again, I'll have you shot!"

In the middle of this mayhem, Brod and I don't move a finger. We're much too weak to climb down and run. We watched the air raid like it was a scene in a film that had nothing to do with us. The airplanes' guns killed only three comrades in our car. The Jews who ran into the fields and the Russians were not as lucky—half of them are dead.

The track is broken. We must all climb down after all. The SS commander asks the old reservists to sort us by nationality. There are French, Polish, Russian, and Czech war prisoners. And the Jews. We know what he wants to do—kill the Jews. Brod and I, as well as all the other Jews who came from France, try to go with the Frenchmen. We know when to seize an opportunity. That's why we've survived until now. The Frenchmen push us away.

"You're not really French. You're Jewish!"

What can we do? I decide to become Polish again. I should have guessed it: the Poles are more brutal than the French.

"Scram, you shitty Yid! Go with the other Yids!"

So I end up with the Jews after all. If the Germans shoot us, I'll die right away. If we have to walk, I'll die of exhaustion later.

Religious Jews begin to say their prayers. One of their faces seems familiar. Where have I seen this guy? Hey, this is Gelber! He mumbles while reading a prayer book. I can't believe it. . . . I saw him as naked as a worm every day when we took a shower after the mine. If he had owned a book, I would have known it. I realize that this is the first book I have seen in three years. How did Gelber (if this religious Jew is indeed Gelber) find a prayer book? I look at this question from every angle, but my weary mind can't find an answer.

They line us in rows of five. It is a trick. They want to convince us we're going on a march, the better to slaughter us. Several comrades try to run away. The soldiers shoot them down like rabbits. We resign ourselves to our fate. We obey the soldiers and follow the tracks. Over the first two or three hundred feet, the rails are broken after the air raid, or bent and twisted as if they were made of tin. Then the tracks are okay again. A freight train comes for us. They lock us inside closed cars, without even the tiny openings of the cattle cars. We suffocate. Some clever comrades pull small pieces of steel, which they "organized" in Krähwinkel, out of their pockets. They begin to widen the tiny gaps between the floorboards. We work in turns. A guy I don't know suggests we escape together.

"They won't catch me. I'll go west and meet the Americans. Are you coming?"

"Look at me. I wouldn't get very far."

After several hours, we remove a piece of wood, so at least we can breathe. We go on working and dislodge a couple more boards. Comrades climb into the opening and drop under the train, which is not moving fast. If I stuck to my principles, I would do it, too, but I can't. They hold on to the floor with their arms and slide down slowly to control their fall. I am too weak to even try. I have no more willpower. I'm waiting for the end.

I won't be able to narrate my adventures to my son. My comrades are dying silently around me. When the train finally stops (where is it going? to Pitchipoï?), whoever opens the door of this car will find only corpses inside.

A comrade is too close for comfort.

"You're sticking your elbow into my ribs, man! Stop banging your head on my back!"

He doesn't answer. I turn toward him and shake him. I was talking to a dead man.

CHAPTER 29

They say "ghetto"

The train stops, the door of our car opens. We are not all dead. Out of two thousand comrades who left the Jawischowitz mine, two hundred are still alive.

I hear vague calls or shouts. Do they say "gâteau"*? No, it is "ghetto." What does it mean? I crawl as slowly as a snail and tumble down from the car. Although my strength is gone, there is still some curiosity left in me. We are not in a camp, but in a city. It may have been a garrison long ago: the tall buildings that line the street look like barracks. Jews who are not as thin as skeletons, who wear a yellow star but no number, welcome us and help us. They carry the sick away on stretchers. I see no SS, no dogs, no kapos.

What's really strange is that these Jews with a yellow star are old. I mean, really old. In Auschwitz, we called a

---

*Cake.

man of forty *der Alter* (the old one). There was no way he could survive.

Our hosts are troubled because nobody told them we were coming. They open a kind of large basement for us. Tiny windows, close to the ceiling, let a little light in. We ask them where we are.

"The Germans call this place Theresienstadt, but its real name is Terezin. Before they invaded, it was Czechoslovakia."

"They created a model ghetto here. They needed it to show the Red Cross how well they treated the Jews."

"They shot a propaganda film. Suppose someone in the French government asked them where the Jews had disappeared. They could show the film. But I don't think anybody ever asked."

"As soon as the film was ready, they put all the actors on a train. We don't know where it went."

We tell them that we know.

We lie down on the cold ground of the basement. The old Jews lock the door and go away. Only now do we discover that a dull pain, which the fear of death had hidden so far, keeps us from sleeping. We're starving! We haven't eaten anything for several days. When will the old Jews come again? After an hour or so, we decide to go out and see. We hoist a shaky chair on top of a dusty table. Not so long ago, my wasted body was waiting for death in a freight car. Now it climbs up on the table and the chair, opens a window, and crawls outside. Three or four other acrobats follow me. We explore a paved court, find a long wooden shed, open a door. . . . The shed is full of clothes and suitcases.

"This is Canada!" one of my comrades exclaims.

I had worked in a clothes room in Auschwitz. Later, the SS built a much bigger one, where the clothes, toys, and violins left on the trains by a million Jews were sorted. The prisoners called this place Canada, nobody knows why.

Instead of undoing the seams of the jackets to find diamonds, we look for food. We find shiny surgical tools, paint tubes and brushes, sewing machines that remind me of my mother. At last, under a mountain of woolen pants: potatoes! Then elsewhere in the shed: carrots, turnips, leeks, onions. As we head back to our window, I see Brod peering out of it.

"You know, Wisniak, this place must have been a school or some institution where a lot of people lived. We've found a big kitchen at the end of the basement, with gigantic cooking pots."

"Is there water?"

"Yes. At least five sinks."

"Then we'll cook a soup!"

We cut and slice the vegetables as fine as we can so they'll cook faster. We do not bother peeling them. In fact, we are so hungry that we could eat vegetable peels. We find wood, matches, bowls, spoons. Fifteen of us share this feast.

"Say, Wisniak, do you remember camping on the banks of the Marne River?"

"Very dimly. As if it had happened in another life. . . . I do remember that the soup wasn't as good as this one. Far from it!"

Our soup's aroma seems to revive other comrades. We tell them where we found the vegetables. Just then, the old Jews open the door of the basement and bring warm potatoes. They're not half as tasty as our soup!

The old Jews are surprised to see that we have already found the stockroom full of clothes.

"Even yesterday, you couldn't have gone there, because of the SS. They vanished last night."

The ghetto's leaders show us dormitories we can use. There are empty buildings everywhere. Their inhabitants have turned into wisps of gray smoke that rose into the sky above Auschwitz. We regroup according to the countries we'll soon go back to. I share a dormitory with fifty Jews who came from France. I see Gelber again. There's a question I want to ask him. "Where did you find your prayer book?"

"Do you remember the infirmary in Krähwinkel? Gamkhi, the Greek doctor, gave it to me. He had taken it from a poor dead guy."

I find Gamkhi in the ghetto's infirmary. He isn't there as a doctor, but as a patient. He seems very happy to see me:

"Ah, Wisniak, I must thank you. You saved my life!"

"Me? I saved your life?"

"Yes, in the freight car. I had a fever, I was half-conscious.

You saw that some of the guys were smothering me. You pulled me away and propped me under some kind of ledge where I could breathe. . . ."

"You know, that's strange, I don't remember it at all."

. . .

The comrades in my dormitory could also benefit from a stay in the infirmary. They're all quite ill. Our old enemy, diarrhea, is tormenting us. I seem to be the healthiest one: at least I can crawl as far as the toilet. After a few days we each receive a ten-pound parcel from the Red Cross. We don't need a doctor to tell us that eating an entire dry sausage in our condition is dangerous, but hunger overwhelms our good sense. We swallow the whole parcel in minutes. As a result, our diarrhea gets worse. The corridor that leads to the toilet is as full of shit as the septic tank I threw Fat Yatché's goat into.

"Can you help us?" I ask the old Jews. "Maybe you could offer a little something to the guys willing to clean up this mess."

"We can offer bread and coffee."

For a few minutes, we picture ourselves drinking real coffee. It's the usual brown water, of course, but it still tastes delicious.

Four or five days after we've arrived in Theresienstadt, they bring men in on stretchers. We recognize the comrades who escaped through the floor of the railway car.

"We hid in a hut," they say. "When we wanted to move on, we found that we were too weak. A peasant discovered us. We thought we'd be shot. But no, a truck came, full of stretchers. They said they'd take us to the best place for Jews."

CHAPTER 30

On May 8, 1945, we hear that the war is over

We find a radio set in a suitcase in the clothes shed. On May 8, 1945, we hear that the war is over. All the comrades who can stand gather in the courtyard. The war is over! We survived! We feel like drinking champagne, singing, dancing with glee. . . . Suddenly, bursts of gunfire spray the courtyard. Some SS haven't left, it seems. The bullets come from a distant building. These last shots break a few windows and wound several old Jews.

It would be stupid to die today. We return to our dormitory and wait until we feel safe.

The next morning, we hear motorbikes. We look out of the window. Russian soldiers! They give away chocolate bars, cigarettes, bacon. This time I'll be careful. Yesterday's bullets didn't kill me; now, I don't want diarrhea to do the job. I just nibble on some dry biscuits.

According to a rumor, the Russians say we are so sick

that they need to quarantine us. Spend more weeks here? I want to move, to cross borders, to see Rachel and Élie as soon as possible. On May 10, I start southward on the Prague road with Brod and three other comrades. We meet six more comrades on the road. We do not walk as fast as we did when the SS encouraged us with their whips and their dogs.

"Tell me, Wisniak, is Prague far from here? What do you think?"

"One of the old Jews told me fifty miles."

"We'll never make it. We'd better stay in the ghetto and wait for the Russians to drive us there."

"Look, we're lucky . . . !"

A horse cart is coming. A well-dressed woman drives the two horses. She's no peasant. We stop her and ask her where she's going. We speak Czech, a language similar to Polish, but she doesn't seem to understand. We expected it, since she's heading away from Prague and toward Germany. We switch to German.

"Are you fleeing Prague before the Russians come?"

"Leave me alone, you scum!"

She threatens us with her whip. Brod laughs.

"There are some Soviet soldiers nearby. Would you like us to take you to them or would you prefer to give us your cart? In which case, we'll let you go free. . . ."

Her face turns quite white when Brod mentions the Soviet soldiers. She steps down and runs away! We are delighted with our luck, we slap each other on the back, we jump into the cart.

"Hey, what's wrong with these horses?"

"They don't want to go back to Prague."

"German horses?"

"Giddap! Hop! Hop!"

"They're just exhausted."

While my comrades are clicking their tongues and shouting, I remember I worked in a stable.

"Let me give it a try, men. . . ."

I slacken the reins and I speak to the horses softly, tenderly, in Polish, while patting their necks—just like I used to when I prepared an oat-and-potato mush with my brother Anschel for the horses in our courtyard. They agree to turn around and walk toward Prague. The others applaud me and elect me to be the driver. The poor beasts have probably eaten nothing since Prague. They were not very strong to begin with. As we say in Yiddish, "The cart rests in winter, the sleigh in summer, the horses never. . . ."

I often ask my friends to step down and walk. Me, I am the driver, so I remain on my seat like a prince!

After a few hours, we meet some Czech underground fighters. When they see our emaciated faces, our bulging eyes, and our striped pajamas, they can tell who we are.

"This road is dangerous," they say. "We're looking for groups of SS. There are also Russian deserters who could attack you. You should turn left after the bridge and hit the main road. Look, here are some armbands. With these on, nobody will bother you."

On the main road, we pass long columns of German soldiers flanked by Russian guards. They don't resemble yesterday's Germans, so proud and so stiff in their beautiful uniforms. They look tired and dejected. They're dirty. Fear distorts their faces. They shuffle their feet. They're not used to walking thirty miles. They're so weak that they can't carry their bags anymore, so they leave them on the side of the road.

"Say, men, we need to feed the horses. Let's look inside the Germans' bags. We may find some nice things, which we can trade for oats in the next village."

You'd think these German soldiers looted the city of Prague. In their bags we find gold jewelry, sheets, brand-new clothes. I find a bag full of striped costumes similar to ours, except they're woolen and quite thick. In what kind of camp did prisoners wear these? And why would a German soldier carry them? I exchange my old torn clothes for one of these gorgeous pairs. I don't want to wear civilian clothes. I want the world to see us as we are. Otherwise, the good people who abstained from helping us during the war might forget we even existed.

When he sees me, Brod laughs.

"You nearly fooled me. I was wondering who the new guy was. This reminds me of a story. The rabbi's disciple, you know—"

"What rabbi's disciple?"

"He spends the night in an inn with his master. The innkeeper wakes him up at dawn because he must take a train. He dresses in the dark, so as not to disturb the rabbi's sleep. He is a clumsy guy, so he picks up the wrong clothes. He runs to the station. There is a mirror near the ticket booth. He doesn't recognize himself. 'This innkeeper is such a fool,' he laments. 'He woke up my master instead of me. So now I'm still asleep in the inn and I'll miss my train!' "

We show our bounty in the first village. The villagers are willing to trade, although our looks frighten them somewhat. The kids keep their distance. They ask their parents whether we are ghosts. The villagers prepare a thick soup for us. One of them looks at our horses.

"Feeding them won't be enough. They need to rest overnight."

We sleep in a stable and start again in the morning.

We pass new processions of German prisoners. We can't help calling them shitbags, Hirenzine, pigs' asses. At sunset, as we are approaching Prague, we see several hundred prisoners resting on the side of the road. Brod is furious.

"These gentlemen are sitting on the grass! Did they let us rest? When we were tired, they offered us eternal rest!"

He runs toward them and shouts: "Are you tired, shitheads? Get up! Kneel! Get up! Kneel! Faster!"

It warms our hearts to see hundreds of tall Germans obey a tiny Jew wearing striped rags. I wonder whether their submissiveness is due to guilt or to fear. Guilt? What guilt? One thing is obvious at least: like the villagers, they know exactly who we are and where we come from. On May 11, 1945, all the people we meet know very well. In a few years, though, they'll say they never heard of camps where Jews were exterminated.

In Prague, gigantic Russian women soldiers, who direct street traffic, point us toward a center for French prisoners. The cooks welcome us like saviors.

"Your horses are just what we need, fellas. We were beginning to be very hungry. The cupboard was bare!"

We enter a drugstore because we see a scale inside. Brod weighs sixty-eight pounds. I weigh seventy-seven.

"Say, Wisniak, you put on weight!"

"You remember, in Theresienstadt, when I cleaned all the shit in the corridor? The old Jews gave me extra food to thank me."

"In Paris, I'll gorge myself. Oh boy! I'll catch up with you and even overtake you, believe me . . . .!"

CHAPTER 31

Hitler didn't kill everybody

Once more, we're traveling in a cattle car. Except this time the door is open, which makes a hell of a difference. We take turns sitting at the door, with our legs hanging outside, just for the fun of it. The Red Cross gives us water and canned meat whenever we stop in a station. I decline the meat and ask for biscuits. I nibble them slowly to reeducate my digestive tract.

There is so much destruction that the train takes several days to reach the French border. We're relieved to be alive but worried when we think about our families. Rachel sent me three letters and three parcels. Then no more. Is it because the Germans decided we'd received enough mail, or has something happened to her? The closer we get to Paris, the darker Brod's face becomes.

"You, Wisniak, your wife was French. Besides, one child

is easy to hide. Mine was Polish, and we had four kids. Do you think a woman with four kids could escape the Germans?"

After we reach the border, we do not see the Red Cross in the stations anymore, but instead there are women who offer us tea and cakes. These women speak French! I barely remember that language. Otherwise, I would tell them that everybody would certainly prefer coffee and buttered bread.

I am coming to Paris in a train—just like in May 1929, exactly sixteen years ago. We pass orchards with blooming trees. The flowers seem to sneer at me: "So you're back? How long will you stay this time?"

Buses take us from the station to Hôtel Lutétia, which serves as a welcoming center for concentration camp survivors. Nurses wash us and disinfect us. Doctors examine us. We have to answer questions: "When were you arrested? In what camps did you stay?"

They serve a light meal. Brod doesn't want to eat.

"I want to see my wife and kids. They've grown, of course. I hope I'll recognize them."

After we fill out some papers, they let us go. A crowd of women and children is waiting in front of the hotel. Although I look carefully, I don't see Rachel and Élie. Brod is livid.

"You see, Wisniak, you lost your wife and your son. . . . Me, I lost my wife and my four little ones."

"They can't come to this hotel every day. Hitler didn't kill everybody. I'm sure they're alive. Let's go to my place, then I'll go with you to yours."

My concierge (doorkeeper) smiles broadly when she sees me. This is a good sign. I thought I had forgotten all my French, but some words come back.

"My wife? She alive?"

"Of course, Monsieur Wisniak. Yesterday she went to that hotel looking for you, but this morning she went to the countryside to fetch your boy."

We go to Brod's apartment. A stranger in slippers opens the door. He stares at us as if we were beggars asking him for money.

"I signed a lease for the apartment," he says. "There's nothing I can do for you."

He understands perfectly who Brod is, but he doesn't seem very happy to see him. Brod becomes even more upset. He is not "as white as a bedsheet," but rather as gray as his pajamas.

"They may have moved, Brod. Do you know anybody else?"

"My sister. . . ."

"Where does she live?"

"Not far."

Brod's sister is a little round lady with red cheeks. Before we ask her whether Brod's wife and children are alive, her solemn look answers the question.

I leave Brod with his sister and walk back home. The concierge has a key to my apartment.

"If you want, I'll bring you dinner, Monsieur Wisniak."

"Thank you, madame. You very nice."

Who is this monster who grabs his steak with two hands and devours it, who throws potatoes like candies into his wide open mouth? Is it me? Monsieur Wisniak? I must not eat too much. Nibbling biscuits is all right. Eggs and onions. . . . The French cook in Prague: "A juicy horse steak, nothing better to perk you up, man!" If I wasn't so tired, I would go down and ask the concierge for a cup of coffee. Real coffee. . . . The lice followed me all the way from Krähwinkel, even though the nurses in Hôtel Lutétia washed me and disinfected me. Shitty bugs. *Krähwinkel* means "the crows' corner." They should call it *Lauswinkel*, the lice's corner. If I lie down in the bed, the lice will settle there. But I am too weak to go on standing up. . . .

I lie down on the living-room floor and I fall asleep instantly. In the middle of the night, I feel somebody shaking me. Brod? Dawn call? My shoes! Where are my shoes? I need my shoes for the sport session!

"Maurice, Maurice . . . It's me!"

A woman. Neither the concierge nor Brod's sister.

"Rachel?"

"My name is not Rachel anymore, but Renée. And our son has become Charlie."

A small boy hides behind the woman. He is scared, like the children in the Czech villages. With my shaved skull, my eyes popping out of their sockets, my gray skin, I look like a vampire.

Rachel (or Renée—I'll have to get used to it) pushes the boy toward me.

"Don't be shy, Charlie. This man is Maurice. Your papa!"

"Let him be. Better he doesn't come close. I'm full of lice. . . . Tell me, hmm, Renée, I would like to ask you something. Can you make a cup of coffee?"

"Coffee? Of course."

I am home with my wife and my son. I drink real coffee. I hope I am not dreaming. A large indistinct crowd is shuffling around in my head—all the comrades who won't drink coffee anymore. Stranger yet, the cup seems to be talking. "Things are as before," it says. "Don't I taste the same? You died and now you're reborn. You're getting a respite, a few more years. Sipping a cup of coffee in Paris in May. Isn't life worth living after all? The woman and the child are not going to the gas. She won't strangle him. You should be happy, believe me."

After putting Charlie to bed, Renée tells me what happened:

"Did you hear about the great Vél d'Hiv roundup?"

"Yes. We went to Auschwitz the next day."

"They came here. A French cop and a German civilian.

Do you know what? They were looking for you! I told them they had taken you to Pithiviers eight months before. The German said, 'In that case, well . . .' He was ready to go, but the Frenchman wanted to arrest us. The German was surprised. 'Why do you want to take them? We have a warrant for the husband, not for the wife and baby.' This German guy saved our lives."

"I thought they only arrested foreign Jews."

"That's what they said. But this swine of a French cop was going to take us away. They wanted to show their German masters they were good pupils. I left Paris to hide with the child. In this neighborhood, everybody knew I was Jewish. I wore the yellow star, after all."

"Where did you hide?"

"You remember the Parisels? We met them when we went camping. I changed my name. I became Renée Vinard. I took a job with a lawyer as a typist. The Parisels found a woman in the countryside who agreed to keep Élie, whom I renamed Charlie. Other friends gave me shelter. Many helped me. I wore a bunch of keys that opened several safe apartments. I worked for the underground as a courier."

"What about my mother?"

"The day of the great roundup, they also went to her place. When they knocked, she didn't open the door. She was lucky that they didn't break in. Your brother Albert paid a woman who came to get her a few days later and brought her to Montauban, where he lived with your sister, Paule."

"Are they okay?"

"Yes. They came back to Paris. They live in their old apartment."

"And Carole, Jacques' wife?"

"They came on the morning of July 16 and they said, 'Prepare your things, we'll be back in thirty minutes.' Do you understand? The cops were not all bastards like the guy who came to my place. They were warning her and leaving her some time to flee. But she didn't know where to go, especially with her little Rosette, so she waited for them. One of her neighbors told me all this. They took her away. She never came back."

"She won't come back. Women with small children were gassed as soon as they stepped off the train."

On the following days, I wash and rewash. Not only do the lice torture me, but diarrhea returns and I smell bad. I should have refused the concierge's dinner. I stay home. My mother, my brother, and my sister come to visit me. They seem nearly as shy as my son. They do not dare hold me in their arms. They're afraid they'll break me, as if I had become a fragile doll. They wonder whether it is really me. They speak in low voices, slowly. They try not to mention my ordeal.

Every night, I see the camp in my nightmares. The SS, the whips, the dogs, the Muselmen. I wake up drenched with sweat and I do not understand where I am. Renée doesn't understand, either. She thinks I'm ill. This illness I'll keep all my life.

When Charlie drops a toy, I jump as if I've heard a shot. I get angry. He cries. I think he cries too easily. I must toughen him up, otherwise he won't be able to confront life's hardships.

After a week, I am strong enough to go outside and walk the few blocks to the apartment of Brod's sister. Her eyes are reddish and puffed.

"He's dead. When you left, he went to my bedroom and lay down on the floor. He didn't move. He didn't want to eat anything. He thought so much of his wife and children that I could feel their presence in the room. I was scared. I called a doctor who gave him some shots. This didn't help. The day before yesterday, when I woke up, I found his lifeless body. Lying on the floor, all curled up. He looked like an Egyptian mummy."

I feel as if my legs are turning to marshmallow. I sit on a chair. Tears run down my face.

"Your brother was a great man. He saved my life. Over there, he never lost hope. He even survived a firedamp explosion in the mine. A large rock protected him. It was a miracle. When we found him, he was sleeping. . . . He told us he hadn't worried too much: 'Either my last hour has come and I'll die, or it hasn't come and I'll live.' In the camp, he wanted to live, to show the SS and the kapos he could resist them. Last week, when he found a stranger in slippers in his apartment . . . I guess he had no more reason to live."

"What about you?"

"I have a six-year-old son. Charlie. I'll live for him."

Author's Note

My father, Lonek Greif, had a blue number tattooed on his arm. Instead of telling me the story of Snow White or Cinderella, he talked about SS, kapos, kommandos, and gas chambers.

In 1950, when my brother Noël was four years old and I, five, he took us camping for our summer vacation. He belonged to an organization, Nature's Friends, that rented a meadow near a beach in Brittany. My mother stayed in Paris to take care of our newborn brother. She didn't like camping, actually.

Our tent neighbors were Maurice and Renée Garbarz. They made leather bags and wallets. They had two boys. One of them, Charlie, was older than me. The other one was younger. His name was the same as mine: Jean-Jacques.

Maurice also wore a blue number on his arm.

My father believed in rough living. He bought eggs at a

farm and showed us how to gulp them down raw. We ate uncooked carrots as if we were rabbits. We didn't complain. We could eat anything. We followed the family food laws: never leave a single crumb on your plate; don't even think of throwing food away. I knew that I was lucky to eat raw eggs on a campground (in French, *camp*) in Brittany while my grandparents, aunts, and cousins had died of hunger in a camp (in French, *camp,* too) in Poland.

Renée took pity on us.

"Look, Lonek, I cooked too many potatoes. If you want some for your kids . . ."

In Paris, Noël and I liked to go and play with Jean-Jacques Garbarz, because he had a Ping-Pong table in his bedroom. The best thing about it was that Renée offered us lemonade. At home, we drank only water.

Much later, Maurice Garbarz, helped by Charlie, wrote a book about his years in Auschwitz: *Un survivant* (Éditions Plon, Paris, 1984). Charlie and Jean-Jacques had graduated from the very best French universities. Charlie worked for the French government as a regulator of insurance companies. Jean-Jacques had moved to America and had become a psychiatrist in San Francisco. He translated the book into English (*A Survivor*. Wayne State University Press, Detroit, 1992).

My elder son visited California in 1992—he was twenty years old. I gave him Jean-Jacques Garbarz's address. It so happened that when my son went to San Francisco, Maurice and Renée were staying with Jean-Jacques. This was their first visit to America. My son already knew an old Auschwitz survivor—Lonek, his grandfather. He said that Maurice, who was then seventy-five, was made from the same mold. "These survivors," my son said, "seem to have more energy and to joke more than ordinary human beings. They're old, but they don't think and speak like old people. I had a lively conversation with him, as if he had been my age."

I saw Maurice and Renée in 1997. They were more than eighty years old and still lived in Paris.

With Maurice's permission, I took his book as a starting point to write this story. I didn't invent any event or situation. I just imagined dialogs and tried to guess what the narrator, whom I called Maurice Wisniak, might think and feel. I went to see Maurice several times with lists of questions. I also saw him once at my father's home. When Maurice met with my father, they always talked about the camp.

"Do you still dream about it?" my father would ask.

"Not anymore. Now at last I can begin a new life!"

"I had frequent nightmares for twenty years or so. Then they went away by and by."

"I used to dream I was back in the camp again. Hey, this is wrong, I thought. I'm sure I got out! Why am I back inside again?"

Maurice's memoirs end in May 1945. The last chapter's title is "Homecoming." When I asked my mother and my father to write their own memoirs, both ended them in

1945, too. I asked my father for an explanation: "That's when my story ends," he said. "Then your story begins." After the war, Maurice Garbarz made handbags during the week, went camping on weekends and in summer. He followed world events and politics and could talk about all kinds of subjects with my son, but when he read books, they were mostly about the camps. He has more of them in his library than anybody else I know. He already has the French version of this book, of course. As soon as the English version is published, I'll send it to him.

While I was working on this story, I discovered that there were many boxers in Auschwitz. Maurice told me about Arie Pach, champion of Holland. Charlie also helped me: he gave me the Auschwitz memoirs of Gabriel Burah, featherweight champion of France.

Primo Levi, an Italian chemist, stayed from March 1944 to January 1945 in Buna-Monowitz, also called Auschwitz III, a camp where slaves were supposed to make synthetic rubber. In his book *If This Is a Man* (one of the very best books about the camps), he quotes one of the strange things that the old numbers told the newcomers on arrival: "Whoever boxes well can become a cook."

A typical boxing event took place in Buna-Monowitz in the fall of 1943. Two professional French boxers, Victor "Young" Perez, flyweight world champion in the early thirties, and Robert Lévy, bantamweight French champion, fought in a real ring against two German giants, a

Wehrmacht soldier and an SS. The commanders of Auschwitz I, Birkenau, and Monowitz were sitting in the first row, the Monowitz barons just behind. In spite of their small size, the professionals would have won easily if they hadn't chosen to be careful and control their punches. As a result, the matches ended in a defeat and a draw. Young Perez and Robert Lévy died in the camp. To survive in Auschwitz, being strong and knowing how to fight did not suffice. You needed lots of luck.